Praise for A Cornisl

CW00661462

'A heart-warming festive tale'
**Cathy Bramley, author of** *The Sunrise Sisterhood*

'Poignant'
**Fiona Lucas, author of** *The Last Goodbye*

'A moving Christmas story about love and redemption that
would melt even Scrooge's heart'
**Phillipa Ashley**, **author of** *Second Chance Summer*

'Absolutely loved this Cornish take on the wonderful Dicken's
classic'
**Angela Britnell, author of** *A Cornish Summer at
Cliff House*

# Also by Liz Fenwick

# A Cornish Christmas Carol

*A Novella*

Liz Fenwick

EMF Press

*For my father, my hero*
*1931–2016*

# Stave One

Abigail closed her laptop. It was dead again. There was no question it was permanent this time. IT would have to sort her a new one immediately. She picked the machine up, balancing it in her hands. It wouldn't take much effort to throw it against the wall. Raising it to head height, she took aim, then frowned when there was a tap on the door. She put it down. 'Come in.'

Sophie Turner, her key researcher and reporter, waddled slightly as she entered. She wasn't really large enough to waddle at seven months pregnant. In fact, she was still barely showing. Sophie used the sway to gain sympathy.

'Abigail, sorry to break this to you so late, but I've just come back from the doctors.' She stopped and Abigail drew her brows together. She would not like what came next.

'I've been forbidden to fly. So I won't be able to go to England tomorrow and complete filming on the last segment.'

Abigail's mouth flattened into a straight line. To think she once thought Sophie had promise, but here she was letting her personal life get in the way of her career. Picking up a pencil, she placed it between her fingers and considered snapping it in half. It would reveal how she really felt about this. Instead, she forced her expression into something akin to a smile and said, 'Of course I understand that you can't take the assignment, Sophie. Doctor's orders and all that.' She swiftly read over the official-looking letter that Sophie passed her.

'I knew you'd understand.' Sophie glanced out of the window behind Abigail. Her body was still tense.

'Of course.' Abigail drummed her fingers on her desk. 'Any suggestions on who can take this on?'

Sophie shook her head. 'Unfortunately none this close to the holidays.' She bit her lip. 'I'm so sorry, I didn't plan this pregnancy, although Tim and I are thrilled.'

'I'm sure.' Abigail twirled her pencil. Sophie was brilliant at what she did, but – and it was a big but – it reminded Abigail why she didn't want a married woman on her team. Pregnancy and childcare ruined the best-laid plans. Now, only weeks before this project was due for completion, she had her top reporter with a baby on the way and doctor's orders not to fly because of a low-lying placenta. Happy bloody Christmas one and all.

'You're from Cornwall.' Sophie smiled, relaxing a little as she warmed to the topic. 'Maybe you could film the last segment and visit some family over the holidays. I can't you tell how upset Tim and I are not to be going. We were going to spend the holidays with my best friend, Jude, who lives there now.'

'I remember.' That had been the start of the whole thing. Sophie's flipping enthusiasm for Cornwall after a visit to her friend Jude last Christmas for her wedding. Fool. Abigail glanced up from her diary, reminding herself that normally Sophie had a brain and quite a good one. Clearly pregnancy hormones had already stolen it. When this entire project was raised, Abigail had clarified that although she thought it was a good idea to make a programme on vanishing cultures, there was no way she would be involved with the section being filmed in Cornwall.

Of course, midway through December with everyone on the production team booked for the holidays, Abigail was faced with going to the one place she had sworn she would never set foot in again. She hadn't been there in seven years, since the last battle with her Aunt Teresa. Abigail supposed she should be pleased that she had held out until she was twenty-seven before she had made a pact with the devil.

Her eyes narrowed. Sophie had suggested this segment to the MD, Trevor, and he, of course, being a Brit too, knew that Abigail was Cornish. He had always sensed her weak spot and knew that she hated the place. The sod was no doubt laughing his head off on the ski slopes of Vail.

Sophie remained in front of Abigail with her hand resting on her abdomen. Didn't she know that the sprog inside her was the end of her career? But Abigail could tell from her serenely smiling face that Sophie didn't care.

'I can see only one solution to this. You'll have to man the office and I will have to go.'

Sophie nodded. 'You'll have a wonderful time.'

'Send me the script, the research, your itinerary and the name of the cameraman.'

'Oh, yes, we have hired someone local who comes highly recommended.'

Abigail rolled her eyes. Local and recommended didn't belong in the same sentence. Anyone with any intelligence or ambition got the hell out of Dodge and never returned. As far as Abigail was concerned, Cornwall was for the nearly dead and the inbred.

'Can you have the travel agent change the flights and the rental car bookings while I make arrangements for Ginge?'

'Sure, and again I'm so sorry, and if you can't get anyone to cat-sit, I'm sure Tim can pop in and feed him. I'm not allowed to go near cats because of toxoplasmosis.'

Abigail sighed. There was no way she would let Tim

anywhere near Ginge. If Becky, the teenager from down the road, couldn't look after Ginge, then she wouldn't go and they could do without this segment of the programme. Who the hell cared about Cornwall and its role in saving Christmas carols? *Cornwall, the Duchy that Saved Christmas* . . . really? Even as a working title it was crap. Plus, she didn't see the segment's appeal to the American populace. But Trevor had overruled her and since he was the one who secured the funding, he made the decisions – the bastard.

This morning she was planning a peaceful holiday at home, and now she had almost finished packing for her flight tonight. Abigail picked up her passport, flipping through it until she reached the photo page. It wasn't a bad photograph, but then she'd been five years younger. She looked in the mirror and touched the bags that had taken up permanent residence under her eyes now. The red-eye flight would add a deeper tint.

Place of birth: Truro. Her passport didn't say that it wasn't in the hospital but in the car on the A390 at rush hour. She had made everyone angry from the start of her life. The tailback went to the A30. It had been Christmas Eve and everyone was desperate to get home. Yet she was named Abigail because she was her father's joy. Her parents had thought they couldn't have any more children. There was a ten-year gap between Abigail and her sister, Jaks.

She snapped the page shut and placed her passport in her bag. Ginge sat with his tail wrapped around his legs, his eyes unblinking. When she looked away, she saw his stealth-move towards her carry-on bag. She smiled as she imagined the customs official's reaction at the other end when a hissing, spitting kitty emerged. 'Why, officer, I have no idea how he could have got in there?'

4

Stroking his head, she scooped him up and nestled him under her chin. 'It won't be long, I promise, and Becky will feed you shrimp on Christmas Day.'

Walking into the kitchen still holding Ginge, she opened a cupboard and pulled out a packet of treats. For once she wouldn't worry about his waistline and would feed him his favourite thing aside from shrimp. He was a cat with the most refined taste. She'd even caught him lapping out of her champagne glass one New Year's Eve as they had watched the ball drop in Times Square on television. She would miss him while she stood in freezing churches listening to choirs sing hymns she didn't want to hear and didn't believe in any more.

Leaving him happily eating, she returned to the bedroom, threw in another cashmere sweater and zipped up her case. Boston might be colder than Cornwall, but the Duchy wasn't as well insulated.

The doorbell rang and Abigail checked to make sure it wasn't the taxi. It was Becky. The gawky teen stood shifting from one foot to the other. Abigail buzzed her in, then opened the apartment door.

'Hi,' said Becky, immediately turning from Abigail to scratch Ginge's head. The girl would go far. She had her priorities right.

'Thanks for doing this at such short notice.' Abigail picked up the spare keys and an envelope containing money.

'I always love looking after Ginge and it means I can escape the insanity of my family for a proper reason.' Becky glanced up.

'Right.' Abigail turned away. She knew that Becky came from a large gregarious family down the road. Abigail did everything in her power to avoid them at all costs, so she wasn't surprised that Becky did the same. 'Here are the keys; you know the alarm code. There's extra money for some treats for Ginge.'

She handed the envelope to Becky. 'If I should be delayed for any reason, I'll be in touch.'

'No worries.' Becky glanced at her. 'Have a merr—' she paused '– productive trip.'

'Thank you.' Abigail heard the taxi on the street. She cuddled Ginge, picked up her bag and left.

Bright lights and tinsel adorned the terminal. Abigail scowled. She was glad she had demanded that she fly business class. Trevor had agreed, chuckling the entire time they spoke. She could have murdered him. She, after all, was giving up her quiet Christmas at home to travel to hell. And the first stage of *Dante's Inferno* was Logan Airport, adorned for the holiday and filled with seemingly happy families who were anything but. Everywhere she turned there was a squalling brat with snot running down its face, or a teenager with headphones on ignoring its parents.

Queues of people snaked around the terminal and she pulled her bag to the business-class line with relief. There were only a few disgruntled travellers in front of her. She flicked through the emails on her phone, which were few; it was clear everyone had skived off early because of how Christmas fell this year. Outside, snow was falling. Maybe it wasn't a bad idea to escape New England when it went crazy for the holidays. Every weatherman was forecasting a seventy per cent chance of a white Christmas. At least in Cornwall Christmas would be appropriately bleak and wet. Whoever wrote 'In the Bleak Midwinter' must have had Cornwall in mind. *Frosty wind made moan . . .*

Stepping up to the counter, she handed over her passport without a word. How could the man behind it take himself seriously? He was wearing a green hat with elf ears and a badge that said 'Jiggle if you're merry'. Seriously, what had happened to appropriate attire and pride? The world had slipped too far down the road of happy holidays and crappy service.

'Could anyone have put anything into your bags without you knowing?'

She raised an eyebrow. How could she believe him a professional when he was dressed like an elf with adult acne? 'No.' But then she thought of the way Ginge had been loitering around her suitcase, nuzzling it, trying to make sure that any other tomcat would know that this was his territory. He might well have dropped a half-chewed cat treat into it while she grabbed her make-up out of the bathroom.

'Is London your final destination?'

She nodded, lying. If it was simply London, all would be fine. London was a fabulous city and she would still be there now, except that this job had proved to be exactly what she had always wanted. Well, not quite. She wanted Trevor's job and in another few years she knew it would be hers. And if not his job, then she'd find something similar, maybe in L.A. From there, it was onto having her own production company and then she wouldn't be stuck filming shitty little segments in quaint ol' Cornwall. Sure, it was beautiful in places; even she could remember the beauty. But it was the one place on earth she never wanted to see again. And why had Sophie remembered a passing comment Abigail had made in her earshot years ago at a Christmas party about some old geezer in Cornwall saving Christmas carols in the 1800s? She had been drunk. Of course she had been, because how else was she to get through an office party celebrating this wretched time of year? Now she made excuses and never attended them.

He handed back her passport with her boarding card. 'Happy holidays!'

Abigail glared at him but didn't say *bah humbug*, although it was tempting. 'Happy holidays' indeed. Hanukkah had been two weeks ago, Diwali ages ago and gosh, wasn't there something called a winter festival for those who thought religion was crap but still wanted a jolly? If you wanted the festivals and the songs then stuff it up and be religious, she thought. If you didn't want the god or gods, then forget the freaking celebrations and nonsense. She glared at the man. She grabbed her briefcase and walked to security, where she knew she would find people as grumpy as she was.

Scoping out the various queues, Abigail tried to avoid the kids and the grannies and went for the one with the most obvious business travellers. They knew how it was done and didn't stand to chat. They got on with it. She turned left and hoped for the best. The X-ray machine to her right had two pushchairs and a family of what looked like ten but could have been more. Had they no self-control? She turned away and extracted her new computer from her bag and slipped off her belt. There were only two people in front of her now.

'Excuse me.'

Abigail ignored the voice, but checked to make sure she had dropped nothing.

'Excuse me.' The voice was louder, but Abigail stepped forward towards the conveyor belt. Only two men stood in front of her. She could be through this particular torture in no time and sitting quietly in the lounge away from the maddening crowds deranged with holiday joy.

She felt a hand on her shoulder and brushed it off.

'Look, I have to get through security. I'm going to miss my flight.'

'So?' Abigail looked at the man.

'I need to go in front of you and these men if they will let me.' He waved his boarding card around.

'Sure, mate, go ahead,' said one of the men.

'That's fine,' said the other.

'No,' said Abigail. 'It's not my problem.' She turned away from them.

'What the . . . ?' He tried to push past her, but she spread her bag to one side and her person to the other.

'You bitch. I'm going to miss my flight.'

She shrugged. 'You should have the left the Christmas party a bit earlier.' He reeked of booze. He tried to go around her again and the man at the front said, 'Look, it's Christmas. Lady, you go first, then he can go after you.' He waved her to the front. She said nothing, but quickly went through security with a look of quiet triumph on her face.

Finally, on the plane and away from the madness of the terminal, Abigail settled in her window seat. The flight attendant who handed Abigail a glass of champagne should have retired twenty years ago, to judge from the grimace permanently etched on her face. The woman had clearly given up on the idea that service was important. Bubbles tickled Abigail's nose and the memory of her first glass of champagne came to mind. She frowned. It must have been the jolly prattle from the captain about the joyous season. Christmas hadn't been a joyous season in a very long time. Someone's phone rang, chiming 'Ding Dong Merrily on High'. If they didn't hang up, Abigail was going to ding-dong them. She wanted to finish this champagne in peace and get the bed flat as soon as they were in the air, but her neighbour clearly had other ideas as he chattered on with the flight attendant.

Knocking back the drink, she reached over the man and handed the empty glass to the flight attendant, who should be checking seatbelts by this stage, not flirting with a man who was half her age. The woman took the glass without a glance and continued chatting until the safety video came on. By then Abigail was grinding her teeth. This overnight, which was a big exaggeration as no one called a flying time of five and a half hours sufficient for much more than a long nap, would only be

9

bearable if she took a sleeping tablet and passed out. She didn't want the next ten days to happen, but they were going to. The best she could make of it was a job done well and fast. The latter was going to be the difficulty unless Cornwall had moved forward into this century in the last few years. It had always moved at a pace slower than a garden snail. Bizarrely, most people thought this was a good thing.

The plane rumbled down the runway and once they were airborne, Abigail slapped on her eyeshades, shoved her seat to full recline and switched the *Do Not Disturb* sign on. Now all she had to do was to wait for the sleeping pill to do its job, and the rest of the flight should be oblivion until touchdown in Heathrow.

*The twilight was softened by the falling snow. I stuck out my tongue to catch a flake, but it melted before I could feel its light, cold touch. His hand held mine, and we swung around with our heads thrown back. Snowflakes chased us as we went round and round until we fell into each other's arms. The world spun as we were motionless, staring into each other's eyes. In the stillness, flake after flake landed on his auburn eyelashes until they melted, looking like tears. They slid down his face to his smiling mouth. Its fullness was touched by a few freckles that had spread from his beautiful skin. I had to kiss him again. If I didn't, this moment of sheer happiness would vanish forever. The world and I held our breath and my heart burst into a million happy pieces. Carols filled the air as a crowd spilled out of a pub. It was too perfect and it couldn't last. Nothing good ever did.*

'Seats upright.' A voice as irritating as possible penetrated the fog in Abigail's brain. 'We are about to land. Tables stored and seats upright.'

Abigail blinked in the light and moved her seat so that the voice would go away.

'Put your window blind up.'

Abigail nearly saluted, but decided that would take too much energy. For a moment she wasn't quite sure where the hell she was, but one look out of the window and she knew it must be England. Nothing was visible except thick cloud. It felt like they were in her head as well. She closed her eyes, but the pain of a broken heart lingered in the space between her brows. She didn't do broken anything these days. Opening her eyes, she focused on a distant point out of the window, willing the fug in her brain to disappear along with images that felt too real to be a dream. Max. Where was he now? Three years ago after too much drink when she was facing her first New England winter she'd dared to search for him online. He too had left Cornwall, for Edinburgh. Max Opie was director of a choral society. Abigail had shut her computer off before she could look further.

Thankfully, she had booked into the hotel at Paddington this morning so she could shower before today's meetings in London discussing future projects. That was hours ago and now it was dark and wet outside as the taxi crawled through the traffic, but bright lights gleamed on every surface. When had London gone so bloody American for Christmas? What happened to British restraint? Even here she was confronted with Santa hats on cashiers. One year she had gone to the Middle East in desperation to escape the bonhomie and found they did the biggest Christmas trees she had ever seen. Then she had tried Christmas in Hong Kong and found it was as over the top as it was in the rest of the world. Christmas was so commercial that countries that didn't believe still joined in the foolish merriment. There was no place sane left on the planet.

In the hotel, the lobby was festooned and the doorman wore a buttonhole of holly. At least that was discreet. Why oh why did Sophie have to be pregnant and sickly? If she insisted on breeding, then she should have had the decency to be able to do her job until she dropped. Abigail hadn't been in front of a camera in years. She much preferred managing things from behind it. On this segment she would do it all except for the filming itself. The CV of the cameraman looked acceptable, at least. He had worked on some seriously good projects and then it appeared he had upped stakes and moved south. The man was obviously lacking in brains.

She glanced at her watch. Damn, she hadn't set it to UK time. Travel mistake number one. Usually her first action on a flight was to set her watch to local time. Thankfully, her phone had automatically switched, and she hadn't missed a meeting. The upside of her mistake was that it was now eight o'clock, and she hadn't realised it. She could go to the bar to kill time until the sleeper train. She might even call a few people here. But then again, maybe not. She didn't want anyone to die of shock. Her last communication with people in the UK, aside from work, had been a birthday card to her nephew. She avoided social media except for LinkedIn. It was all she needed.

Zipping her suitcase shut, Abigail made sure Sophie's notes, her computer and phone were in her handbag. The script still needed work to make it sound genuine, coming from her mouth rather than Sophie's. What worked for a chirpy American would not for a hardened Brit.

One last check of the hotel room, then she headed out to be bombarded by Christmas music. It filled the lift and the lobby. Thankfully, once in the dark bar the music was quieter and the decorations more subdued. She pulled out a stool and sat at the bar.

'What can I get you?'

'A Tanqueray and tonic. Make it a double.'

'Sure.'

She scrolled through her messages. Becky had sent her a picture of Ginge with a Santa hat on. So not funny, and he didn't look too pleased about it. She needed to have words with the girl. Ginge didn't 'do' Christmas unless it was simply turkey and shrimp. He was very partial to the dark meat. He was the only reason she colluded in the whole roast thing. If it had been up to her, they would have had a Chinese take-away.

She placed her new laptop on the bar. The IT geek had grumbled about having to work through the night to transfer data, but he'd done it. And it appeared he'd done a decent job, except he had put MERRY CHRISTMAS in bright bold letters on her home screen and she hadn't yet figured out how to remove it. It was clearly his idea of a joke. The laugh would be on him when she returned and denied his request for vacation or something else. Bloody busybody, putting messages on her screen. She sighed, then pulled up Sophie's notes and scrolled through them. They were somewhat vague, and her hand-written ones weren't any better. Abigail shook her head, wondering how the woman came up with the results she did with such fluffy thoughts. The research was sound, though. Abigail wasn't sure how, after years of performing in the ubiqui-tous Nine Lessons and Carols service as a schoolgirl, she had never known it had all begun in Truro when the cathedral was being constructed in the 1800s. The wily bishop, Edward White Benson, had apparently gathered his flock in a wooden shed. There was an asterisk next to this line. Abigail referred to the notes.

*The esteemed bishop created the service to keep his flock out of the pub.*

She laughed, liking his thinking. 'Scrooge,' she whispered.
The bartender looked up. 'Another drink?'
She shook her head and focused on the screen. She would be filming at a re-creation of the original service. Joy. If this was the case – and a quick look at the schedule confirmed it – she

would need more information. The intended audience in the States might not be familiar with Nine Lessons and Carols. She sipped her drink and made a note to add information about King's, Cambridge, the college now most associated with the service.

She opened the schedule again. The notes might have been lacking, but the appointments and locations were concrete. However, it was only a list with their first name and a phone number. Not even an email address. How did Sophie work like this?

Tomorrow afternoon at two o'clock she was due at the cathedral for the final dress rehearsal of the recreation, which would be performed on Boxing Day. Max was the contact. *Max* was written everywhere. Max who? *Max*. Abigail took a deep breath and slowly released it. Hah. Plenty of people were called Max, but few were called Maximilian Arthur Opie. It wouldn't be the same one she had once known, but whoever this Max was, she had an appointment with him on Christmas Eve at Manaccan Church near the Helford River. The Max of her past wouldn't be in some far-flung forgotten church in Cornwall. Even if he had left Edinburgh, he would be teaching at some worthy school encouraging children to believe in music and its power. She shook off thoughts of the past. It must be the prospect of being in Cornwall that had brought those deliberately forgotten moments to the fore.

Pushing Max to the back of her mind, she highlighted the car rental pickup at Truro train station, where she would also meet the cameraman and shoot some exterior shots before filming the rehearsal. When that concluded she would drive to Manaccan, where she was staying in a farmhouse B&B, as they would also film both the crib service at six and then the midnight Mass at the village church. At least Manaccan was nowhere near where she had grown up; none of the locations that they would film in were. That was the one thing she could be grateful for. Not even her job would make her go anywhere near there again.

But Max. She sipped the gin and tried not to think about him, wherever he was now. Would his mouth have lost some of its fullness? Would those hazel eyes be any less soulful? Maybe he was married with five kids. No, that would be quick work by anyone's standards. Even if he had met someone immediately, it was only eight years. Calling up the browser on her laptop, she typed his name into the search box.

She had resisted googling him for years, and that was still the right thing to do. Letter by letter, she deleted his name. She did not want to know what happiness he had or hadn't found. He belonged to the past and he would stay there.

However, there was another name that came to mind. Freddie. It had been five years. No, it had been seven since she had spoken to him. Abigail wasn't sure she should call him, but then at the moment she seemed inclined to do things that she wouldn't normally do in her right mind, like google Max. Maybe it was jet lag or the threat of returning to Cornwall. She would only be in the Duchy for ten days and most of the time she would be working. Would Freddie even want to speak to her? In order to ensure he would have what she had been denied, she had agreed to cut all contact. The last time she heard his voice, he was ten. He would be eighteen now and wouldn't need her. He was an adult. No doubt he would have forgotten her by now. But maybe the evil aunt had let the birthday cards through. She pressed her tongue against her teeth, forcing the rise of emotion away.

Her phone sat on the bar next to her gin. She reached out but stopped. Her hands – despite her care of them – had aged so much since she'd last held him, so long ago. What was he doing now? Did he still look like Jaks? She swallowed. The phone flashed as an email came in. Why should she call Freddie? Because she was in the same country? No, she wouldn't call. He knew how to reach her if he needed her. There was no sense in stirring the old woman's wrath. She'd done that often enough. Besides, Freddie's inheritance wasn't safe until Teresa was six feet under. She pushed her phone away. Then it rang. The number on the screen was a UK one, and one she didn't recognise. Maybe it was the cameraman. 'Abigail Scorrier.'

'Abby,' a deep voice said.

She frowned, she hadn't used Abby in years.

'It's Freddie – Alfred – your nephew.' The voice sounded so deep, so grown-up. Her hand shook as she ran her finger through the condensation on her glass.

'She's dead.'

She picked up the gin and took a big gulp.

'Did you hear me? Aunt Teresa is dead.'

'Yes.' She knocked back the rest of the drink and indicated to the bartender to give her another one. 'When?'

'Last night. I tried to reach you.'

'I was on a plane.' She couldn't make the voice she was listening to match the picture of Freddie she had in her mind.

'Where are you?'

'London.' She took a deep breath. 'Where are you?'

'Home.' He cleared his throat.

'You OK?' Abigail couldn't associate the voice speaking to the child she'd known. There was silence on the other end of the phone.

'Can you come?' His voice wavered, giving a hint of the boy she'd known.

'When's the funeral?' she asked.

'I don't know yet. There's so much to do and I've just arrived.'

'Arrived?'

'I was still at uni trying to finish up some stuff before the holidays.'

It was the twenty-third of December and he had still been at university. That wasn't good, was it? Over the years, they had assured her he'd been well loved. What had happened to the child she'd left behind? Where was he at uni? What was he studying? 'Keep me informed.'

'Is that all you can say?' His voice faded away.

'I'm sorry.' She thought of all the things she could say, and none of them were polite. Anger rose in her and she tasted the bile her aunt had always brought up in Abigail's stomach. That woman had in one way or another taken everything from her.

'OK. You now have my mobile number. You know how to reach me.' He hung up.

Abigail leaned back. The bitch was dead. But it was too late to change anything.

*Clinging sand washed away by cold water and giggles. A small hand gripped mine tightly as we paddled at Gwithian, watching the surfers chase the perfect wave. The fair head dropped and tugged my arm as he bent down to pick up a stone, then lifted it to me. My heart exploded with a love I didn't know I could feel for a child, my sister's child and now mine. Freddie.*

*'Abby, this is my treasure.' He held the rock out. It was nothing special, a bit of red serpentine that came from the Lizard Peninsula at some point or other. Serpentine was more common on the eastern beaches than these, and so it stood out on the sands of Gwithian. Maybe that's what made it special to Freddie.*

*'It's beautiful, love.'*

*'I want to give it to Mummy.'*

*I took a deep breath. 'Of course. We can stop and visit her on the way home and you can tell her all about your day.' Not a day passed that he didn't want to visit his mother's grave. Each time, my soul bled. The world was too cruel. I scooped him up in my arms and swung around and around until we were both dizzy and collapsed on to the sand, laughing.*

'I love you, Abby,' he said.

Breathing in his scent of chocolate and sea pray, I said, 'I love you too, Freddie.'

'Will you love me always?' he asked.

'Always.' I rested my forehead against his.

'Promise?' He pulled back and opened his eyes wide, focusing on me.

'Promise.'

'Cross your heart?'

I did, and he relaxed.

'Don't leave me like Mummy did.'

'I won't do that.' I clutched him close and prayed.

Freddie. He was in university. Teresa was dead. Abigail had a job to do: film a couple of choirs, speak to a choirmaster and a Cornish-language expert, and wax lyrical about a place she hated. Just your average work week. She paid the bill and headed to the train via the store to collect a few essentials for the journey.

Paddington Station was quiet compared to when she'd come through this morning, now almost eerie as a startled pigeon flew past her. Despite the festive music tinkling over the tannoy, there was no jollity. It was nearly ten-thirty and she could either board the train or go into the first-class lounge. Abigail hesitated. People were chatting and the noise of laughter slipped out from under the door. She turned instead and sought her carriage on the *Night Riviera*. It always sounded so romantic, but it was so far from it. It would be a night spent listening to the train chugging at speed, then pulling into sidings. She knew it well from old, when she would commute each weekend to be with Max. Bittersweet, and she didn't do sweet anything. Bitter was far better. Now the sleeper was purely a means to an end – reaching Cornwall without losing an entire day in the process.

The guard walked down the platform to greet her. 'Hello, my lover.'

Abigail flinched. Was she already in Cornwall?

'Have you booked a berth?'

'Yes.' Abigail handed over her ticket.

'This way, my dear.' Abigail followed the woman down the narrow corridor that lined the cabins. 'What would you like for breakfast? Tea? Coffee? Muffin or a bacon sarnie?'

'Only coffee, please.'

'You sure, my dear?' The woman glanced up and down Abigail's slight frame.

'Yes.'

'Very well. We arrive in Truro five past seven. I'll come by at six-thirty, unless you'd like me to wake you earlier.'

'That's fine.' Abigail doubted that she would get much rest on the train anyway. She didn't sleep well and hadn't for years. Sleep, unless she took a pill, meant dreaming: dreaming about things that hadn't and couldn't happen. It was wasted time, and she knew all about that. Besides, the dream from the plane had haunted her all day.

The guard left her in peace and Abigail changed into her PJs and opened the canned premixed gin and tonic she'd bought in the dodgy convenience shop across from the hotel. Propped up in the bunk, she scrolled through her emails as the train pulled out of the station. She sniffed the plastic cup and decided that tinned gin and tonic without fresh lemon and ice left a great deal to be desired. Should she change into her clothes and go to the bar? She frowned. Why not go in her PJs? They were decent. In fact, they were stylish . . . black silk. She swirled the liquid and decided, what the hell. She no longer knew anyone here, so why not? Slipping on her high-heeled black boots, Abigail left her cabin and tried to walk in a straight line as the train built up speed. Her heel caught on the hem of the silky bottoms and she crashed into a door.

'Hello?' a voice called, sending a shiver of recognition up her spine. She shook it off as foolishness.

'Sorry,' Abby mumbled as she picked up her pace towards the lounge car. At the door she noted the tired but festive look of the passengers and staff. It was the night before Christmas Eve and normally sane people had lost all reason. There was even a woman wearing flashing antlers and a red nose. Abby was sure her nose had to be as red underneath its cover as it was on top. If she were to make a documentary of the foolish fantasies of Christmas joy, here would be a brilliant place to begin. The imaginary camera in her head panned through the carriage. There was the man who had obviously been on his Christmas lunch with his colleagues and finished the bottle of port with them. His face matched his drink. Next was a woman in a sparkly dress that belonged in a disco, not on the sleeper train to Cornwall.

Abby weaved through the people to the bar. Her PJs were positively tame; she needn't have worried. She smiled at the man in uniform behind the counter. He had a sprig of mistletoe above his name badge. Was she supposed to kiss his chest?

'Could I have a gin and tonic to go?'

He frowned. 'To go?'

Shit, she'd been living in the States for too long. 'To take away.'

He smiled and went to work. She hated Christmas almost as much as she hated Cornwall, and now she was facing them both together. 'Make that a double.'

'OK.' Eventually he turned, grinning, and handed over two small bottles of gin and a can of tonic with a cup containing two cubes of ice and a slice of lemon.

She pursed her mouth, thinking about saying something rude, but that wouldn't help. 'Could I have more ice, please?'

He piled two more cubes into the plastic cup.

'Thanks.'

'Happy Christmas.'

She raised an eyebrow. 'Whatever.'

She started to leave the lounge car when, out of the corner of her eye, she caught a flash of auburn hair behind a group of teenagers all wearing tops proclaiming them the Cornish Carol Singers. Her breath caught. Once she had known someone with hair exactly that colour. She turned away quickly and stepped aside as the teens began singing 'God Rest You Merry Gentlemen'. They all wore antlers and carried several buckets labelled with a homeless charity. The people sitting in the lounge car joined them and Abigail wanted to put her hands over her ears.

She couldn't get past as they blocked her passage back to the safety of her cabin. Applause echoed in the carriage as they finally came to the last note.

'Thank you, all. We've been singing in Trafalgar Square to raise money for the homeless at Christmas and now are on our way back to Cornwall. Don't suppose we could sing you another song and you could contribute?' A petite blond girl spoke.

'Sing on,' shouted a man reaching for his wallet.

Fools, thought Abigail. These kids will spend the money in the bar once the codgers have gone to bed.

'Make it a Cornish one and you can have twenty quid,' said a man holding a can of beer.

'You're on.' A tall spotty young man blew into a pitch pipe and they began singing 'While Shepherds Watched Their Flocks' to an old Cornish tune, 'Lyngham' by Thomas Jarman. A lump lodged in her throat. It had been years since she'd heard this and tomorrow she would film it, and again on Christmas Day, then again on Boxing Day. She didn't need to hear it now. She pushed past them with her head bowed, staring at the melting ice in her cup. One of the kids rattled a bucket. She rolled her eyes and dashed down the narrow corridor, unable to get the repeat out of her head and the pure sound of their voices rising.

. . .

With her gin perched precariously against her pillow and her computer on her lap, Abigail delved into Sophie's notes. The was a whole section devoted to the Cornish 'curl' or carol. She sighed. How the Cornish loved their repeats. Like rounds, these emerged from a line being sung by at least two distinct voices or groups. She remembered hearing a story from her schooldays saying it all arose from the men singing in the mines. And thanks to a Cornishman, one Davies Gilbert of St Erth, the world held on to its Christmas carols. In 1822 he published a collection entitled *Some Ancient Christmas Carols and Complete with their Tunes*. Another Cornishman, William Sandys, jumped on the proverbial bandwagon with *Christmas Carols, Ancient and Modern*.

Because of two Cornishmen, the world had to put up with all this forced good cheer. Those meddling men should have it left well enough alone. Without their intervention, it was quite possible that Christmas wouldn't have blown up into the over-sentimental, over-commercialised charade that it was now. It might have faded into gentle obscurity like so many other holidays.

But music was in the Cornish blood like it was in the Irish and Welsh, even though, unlike the other two, the language had been virtually lost and the traditional tunes had been erased from all but a few memories. And thanks to Sophie, Abigail was going to film it for posterity and to feed America's television-watching population's lust for the Duchy since the revival of *Poldark* and the silliness of *Doc Martin*.

Words on the computer screen blurred. Although her body clock told her it was only eight-thirty in the evening, she was exhausted. Her mind was swimming with details of the Cornish carols as she shut the computer down and crawled under the duvet after adjusting the thermostat in the cabin to a higher temperature. She was chilled to the bone.


*I walked into the hall and my mouth went dry. I was the new girl and all these people had been singing in the choir for years. And besides, there were so many hot guys, especially the one with ginger hair grinning at me from the second row. I'd seen him before. He played the piano for the opening assembly. It had been breathtaking, and he was cute.*

*The choirmaster stepped forward. 'I'm so glad you've come, Abby.'*

*'Thank you, sir.'*

*'Stand by Rachel in the sopranos for the moment.' Rachel waved and my stomach tried to settle, but it wasn't doing a good job. Everyone was watching me and judging. Even though everyone seemed OK, they always judged. I was the new kid in the second-hand uniform whose mouth was so dry I wouldn't be able to sing a note.*

*'I know it's only September.' He moved to the piano and played a snippet of the 'Hallelujah Chorus'. 'I know we have several concerts, assemblies and recitals before Christmas but we have been invited to sing Handel's* Messiah *with the massed choirs at the Royal Albert Hall.'*

*I felt all the blood leave my head as happy gasps erupted around me.*

*'Exciting, yes, but it will mean extra practice. Are you all in?'*

*Hands shot up and mine didn't. Not because I was scared – I was – but because all these things had costs associated with them. There was no money, let alone extra for trips to London.*

*'Great, we're going.' He tapped his baton. 'We are short on time, so if everyone would pick up the music on your way out.' He coughed then added. 'If Max Opie and Abby Scorrier could stay behind for a moment ...'*

The choir drifted out of the door and so did the choirmaster, calling back. 'Max, could you run through the basics with Abby to see if she's a soprano or a much-needed alto?'

'Sure thing, sir.' Max smiled as he sat at the piano. My stomach fell to the floor and rolled out the door. I was in love. I wouldn't be able to speak, let alone sing. Up close his eyes weren't plain hazel but had flecks of yellow, orange, green and grey. I looked at my scuffed shoes. There had been no time this morning to polish them. It didn't help that I had a habit of dragging my toes in the ground when I was unsure. This week had been made up of days of feeling unsure, especially about leaving Mum alone in the cottage on the moor.

'Abby?'

I looked up.

'Relax. I don't bite.' He grinned. 'Well, not unless I'm invited to.'

I blushed and looked at the floor.

'Is there anything you want to sing?'

I shook my head.

He played a few scales. 'Do you know where your voice sits?'

I nodded.

'Do you have one?'

I laughed. 'Yes, I think I'm an alto.'

'Brilliant.' He shuffled some music around. 'Do you know 'Honey Bun' from South Pacific?'

'Sort of.'

He slid to the side of the bench. 'Take a look. We performed this last spring.'

I sat beside him. He began to play and his thigh brushed mine. His fingers fumbled on the keys. He stopped playing and turned to me. 'Sorry.'

He was so close I could count the freckles on his cheeks.

'When are you free so I can bring you up to speed on our

*standard pieces?' He stood and held out a hand for me. 'I have to head to physics now.'*

*I put my hand in his and my heart stopped. He pulled me to my feet, and we walked out into the crisp September morning with his hand still holding mine. 'I'm free the period after next.'*

*'Me too. It's a date.'*

*I nodded. He smiled, then whispered in my ear. 'I'm really looking forward to it.'*

*'Me too.'*

*He ran in the direction of the physics lab. I could barely move, my legs had gone so weak.*

The train lurched into a siding, and Abigail woke from a light sleep. Dim illumination from the emergency light cast the cabin in an eerie green glow. High above her feet, the television screen flickered. She blinked. The screen fizzled with wiggly lines and then a moan emanated from the screen, but it couldn't be from there. She stuck a finger in her ear and wiggled it around. The passenger next door must be having a bad dream. The walls of these cabins were far too thin. She had heard him snoring earlier, but she was at least grateful that it wasn't someone trying to get it on. Snoring was bad enough, but listening to people having sex would be a nightmare.

The TV screen lit up again. She frowned and crawled from under the duvet and poked it. It was freezing in the cabin and she was sure she had put the heating on before she dropped off to sleep. Despite pressing the off button on both the television and remote, it remained on, tuned to nothing but static. Abigail wished she could find her eyeshades. That light was going to annoy the hell out of her.

The train's engine stopped. She pulled the duvet up over her head, but then her feet stuck out of the bottom. Abigail tried to curl up on her side. The moaning began again. She made a fist, about to bang on the wall and tell the man – for she was sure it was a man next door – to shut it.

'Abigail Scorrier,' said a voice that sounded an awful lot like her sister.

She sat bolt upright in the narrow berth, clutching the duvet to her chest. The TV screen flashed, and there was her sister's face in close-up. But it wasn't her sister's face because she was, well, ghostly white and, Abby squinted, sort of transparent too. In fact not *sort of*: Abigail could see a Christmas tree with multicoloured lights shining behind her sister's face, giving her something like a bad case of spots or chicken pox.

'Abigail Scorrier.' This spotty apparition sure sounded like her sister.

'Jaks?' Abigail wrinkled her nose. She hadn't spoken to a television screen, had she? She pinched her wrist and stopped her squeal of pain emerging from her mouth.

'Yes.' The head moved, causing the spots to slip into different areas of her face. Not a good look.

'What the f—?' Her sister had been dead for thirteen years. Abigail glanced at the two empty gin bottles. She hadn't had so much to drink that she was hallucinating. Maybe it had been a bad batch. She hadn't needed to take a sleeping tablet, as the history of Cornish singing had been enough to put her to sleep. But looking at the packet, it seemed she had taken one. It must have been automatic, because she had no recollection of doing it.

'Swearing won't help.' Jaks looked down at the empty gin bottles. 'Nor will alcohol and sleeping pills.'

Abigail rubbed her eyes, hoping the ghastly image of her sister on the television screen would disappear. This was some weird nightmare. She hadn't dreamt of her sister in a long time. Jaks had died thanks to an accidental overdose when Abby was twenty-one and in her last year of Oxford, leaving her and her aunt as guardians of four-year-old Freddie.

26

'Well, you should know.'

'I do, now,' said Jaks.

Abigail shook her head. 'It's a bit late.' She thought of the near misses Jaks had had along the way. She should have known better, and she certainly should have taken more care, if only for Freddie.

'Yes, for me it is, but not for you.'

'I'm not an alcoholic and I've never done drugs.'

Jaks raised an eyebrow. 'Don't lie.'

'I'm not.' Abigail crossed her arms.

'No, you're not an alcoholic yet, but you do drugs.'

'No, I don't.'

Jaks' glance fell on the packet of sleeping tablets beside the empty gin bottles.

'It's not the same.' Abigail's voice rose, but then she glanced at the wall. She didn't need her neighbours to wake because she was shouting at a television which contained a weird image of her dead sister.

'Abby, don't try to lie to yourself. It doesn't work. I know.' The disembodied head of her sister lectured.

'You may know, but how the hell did you get into the television on the *Night Riviera* to Truro?'

'I spend my time haunting the tuned-out TVs across the globe, along with millions of other souls with unfinished business.'

'You mean every time I turn my television off some random head hangs out in the space?'

'Yes.'

'No, no, no.' Abigail shuddered, convinced she was dreaming now. 'That is too weird. I don't believe in disembodied heads, or ghosts, or even souls for that matter.'

'That's why I am here before it is too late for you and you suffer the same fate as me.'

'Look, I'm not you. I didn't waste my life. I earned a good

degree. I'm employed and not living off the family money or name.'

'No, but you are wasting your life as much as I did. I, at least, produced one worthwhile thing – Freddie.' The face stopped moving. Jaks' eyes stared directly at Abigail and seemed to look straight through to her non-existent soul. 'What have you done? Can you even say you have developed the people who work for you, or have you simply used them to climb higher?'

Abigail flinched. She was focused and forthright. She did not suffer fools. Everyone had to make their own way, as she had had to.

'Think hard, Abby. You are now thirty-four. Is the world a better place because you are in it?'

'What sort of question is that?'

'An important one. You think I wasted my life, and I did.' Jaks sighed, but it didn't sound right. The breath kind of whooshed through her. Abigail pinched her arm again. She needed to wake up before things became even stranger . . . if that was possible.

'But you have a chance to redeem yours.'

'What if I don't want to?'

'Stubborn to the last.' Jaks shook her head. 'Then your time haunting the blank screens around the globe will go on for ever.'

Abigail saw a shadowy figure move behind Jaks' head, but she could still see the Christmas tree lights. The television screen flickered and Abigail wondered if she would ever shut her television off again. She glanced at the empty glass and the sleeping tablets. Maybe she needed to talk to her doctor about taking something stronger. She didn't want to dream, and she certainly didn't want to hallucinate.

'This is a chance to not end up like me. To make your life meaningful. Your first visitor will appear at one o'clock.'

'What?' More interruptions to what little sleep she would get on this train to hell.

'Be alert and don't waste the chance you have.' Her sister turned and moved away while other faces slipped past, occasionally turning to look at Abigail. She rubbed the goose bumps on her arms as the familiar visage of the grumpy woman who used to run the village shop swept past, staring at Abby with eyes lit by the tree lights behind her head.

The screen went dead and Abby rubbed her temples. What had just happened? Was she awake or asleep?

# Stave Two

## The First of the Three Spirits

Abigail bunched up the pillows and curled into a sitting position with the duvet tucked about her. She'd be lucky if she could fall asleep by the time one o'clock rolled around. But the train began moving again, and soon the gentle sway rocked her to sleep.

*I sat on the edge of the bed looking at Jaks and the tiny bundle in her arms.*

*'Don't be afraid. Alfred won't bite.' She grinned, holding out her son.*

*'He should bite you for landing him with the name Alfred. Seriously, Jaks, what were you thinking?'*

*'We'll call him Freddie and I chose Alfred because of Bateman.' She grinned and pushed the squirming thing that was my nephew into my arms. He wasn't too ugly.*

*'Abby, you have to promise that if something ever happens to me, you'll look after him.'*

*'Don't be silly. What could happen to you?' The baby grabbed my finger and held on tight.*

*Jaks big dark eyes looked at me and sadness filled them. 'I know I've been clean for a year . . .' Her voiced faded away.*

'Freddie is your reason to hold on, here and now.'

Her mouth lifted, but the smile didn't reach her eyes. They were haunted by things she wouldn't say. Mum knew and Aunt Teresa was useless. However, she had paid for Jaks' rehab, as well she should. It was Teresa's money that had bought the drugs in the first place. The evil aunt was all about the money and the house. She always had been. It still surprised me she'd shown Jaks any kindness as, in her eyes, both Jaks and I were bastards since Mum and Dad never married. They'd always meant to, but had never got around to it. They felt it never mattered, but it had, or at least it had to bloody Teresa and to the courts.

I sighed and looked at my tiny nephew. I would help Jaks and make sure both of them had all my support.

'Will you promise me that if anything happens to me you will look after him?'

'Of course I will.' The little fist tightened around my finger. 'I'll do whatever it takes, but that won't be necessary.' I looked at my sister and prayed her demons were behind her.

The sound of the engines had gone, and the shade on the window snapped up. Her eyes flew open. Where was she? In the distance, she heard the chime of a clock. It was one. She had a crick in her neck from sleeping sitting up with her head resting on her chest. Rubbing it, she hoped she wouldn't be forking out for multiple sessions with a chiropractor.

An unseen light illuminated the landscape out of the window, where snow was falling. They must be somewhere cold, like one of the moors. Wind whipped the flakes past the window. She looked at her watch to check the time. It was two minutes past one on 24 December. She stood up, wrapping the duvet about her shoulders, and looked out. Despite the falling snow, she could make out a distant tor. The ground was lightly dusted white, erasing some of the details. She shivered.

'It is beautiful.' A deep voice said from behind her.

She swung around. There was a big man standing in a black

31

velvet cloak not a foot away from her. In fact, he was so close she had to crane her sore neck to see his face.

'Who are you? And what are you doing in my cabin?' Abigail rubbed her sweaty palms on the duvet. It was best never to show fear, she had discovered a long time ago.

'I am the Ghost of Christmas Past.'

'What the . . . ?' She didn't finish her sentence. He was frowning like an old schoolmaster. Clearly the Ghost of Christmas Past didn't do swearing.

'Take my hand and you will see.'

She shook her head. If he thought she was going to touch him, he was totally out of his mind. This was obviously some weirdo who had stayed in the lounge car too long drinking the eggnog. He wore a wreath of holly and ivy about his head and his nose was red, no doubt from the aforementioned eggnog.

'Abigail Scorrier, take my hand.'

'How do you know my name?'

'I am the Ghost of Christmas Past.'

'That doesn't answer my question.' She shivered. How did he know her name? This must be some sort of wind-up. She looked for hidden cameras but saw only the blank television screen where her sister's face had appeared.

'Time is slipping away. Take my hand, Abigail Scorrier.'

His outstretched hand was enormous and reminded her of her father's. The image of Jaks' head and her weird words of warning came to her as she looked from him to the screen. Surely this wasn't real, and if it wasn't, what could possibly happen to her?

She clasped his hand and instantly they were flying through the window out onto the snow-frosted moor. She must remember to read the precautions on the sleeping tablets and their reaction with gin. This was some wacky dream. Normally if they worked, she didn't remember what she'd dreamt about, or if she had at all. It was the sleep of the dead, almost.

He continued to hold her hand as they came to the gates of Scorrier House. The grand pile had been built from her ancestors' successful trade in tin and copper. Abigail's family had only lived in it for eighteen months, but her father had grown up there. He'd had mixed feelings when he'd inherited the house. Not that she understood it at the time. Understanding came later, much later.

The granite piers were decked in a laurel garland, and the circular finials that topped them were wearing Santa hats. She was six, and she remembered her father hoisting her into the air to place the hat on one of the granite balls. Then he helped Jaks do the same with the other. Her mother had stood back, laughing, before taking a picture of the three of them standing in between the gates, holding hands.

Abigail watched as her family strolled along the drive to the house. A large green wreath adorned the front door and lights shone out of every window. It was a legacy from her fear that Father Christmas would somehow miss them.

The four of them, like the tight unit they were, moved into the house, laughing, and she realised this was the Christmas before her father had died.

The ghost placed a large hand on her shoulder and encouraged her to follow them into the house, but Abigail stood still. They had been so happy then and a few days later it would all change. By New Year's Eve, her father was dead and all the troubles began. The ghost propelled her on into the house.

Evergreen garlands festooned the banister leading up to the gallery. From the chandelier, mistletoe hung by a big red ribbon. Scorrier House was made for Christmas, her mother had always said. Each year they had scoured the woods and beaches to find new items to complement their collection of cherished Christmas ornaments that came from their grandmother.

The phone in the hallway rang and her father picked it up. 'Happy Christmas.' The smile on his face disappeared and became neutral. 'Thanks for calling, Teresa. So sorry you couldn't join us, and I'm pleased you've received the hamper from Fortnum's.'

He played with the phone cord and Abby could hear her aunt's dull drone. Whatever she was saying had totally removed the joy from her father's face. Teresa was like that. If there was happiness, she had to trample on it. Abigail watched him place the phone down and come into the drawing room. She and Jaks had moved the piano closer to the tree and Jaks had begun playing 'Silent Night'. He walked up to her and placed his hands lightly on her shoulders. His baritone joined their choir of two. Mum watched and tended the fire.

'We're due down at the pub shortly, but you all sound as if you're in good voice.' Mum stood and joined us.

'How can you not be, at Christmas?' Dad held out his hand for Mum's. He smiled, but Abigail could see now that it didn't really reach his eyes and her mother gave him a searching look. The young Abby grabbed her father's hand and led him into the hallway.

The ghost stopped her from following them as the family walked down the drive and into the village. Abigail remembered how they had sung the entire journey. It had been perfect and only snow had been missing.

The apparition took her hand. They soared above the countryside over abandoned engine houses and mines until the tors of Bodmin appeared, then finally a small lonely cottage. The ground was hard with frost as they walked up the rutted path that made do as a drive. Not that their car could manage it. The furrows were so deep that they would take the bottom off the old car. She realised they'd covered time as well as ground, and she and the ghost stood outside looking in at her ten-year-old self, reading Dickens' *A Christmas Carol* by the fire. Jaks had left home by then, having sided with her aunt after a blazing row with their mother over money or the lack of it. From then on, it had been Abby and her mother. It had been four years since their father had died and their proper home was still intestate. She and her mother were staying in a friend's holiday cottage on the moor.

The winters were bleak and Abby couldn't attend her old school because they had no money. Her aunt had it all, as Abby's father had left no will. Teresa had been living in Scorrier House looking after Abby's grandfather until he died. Teresa had contested her father's will and everything went in her favour when Abby's father died eighteen months after his father.

This whole fiasco had left Abby and her mother penniless; well, except for Jaks, who knew on which side her bread was buttered. Jaks had sucked up to Teresa and received an allowance, a generous one, which proved to be her downfall in the end.

Abby had lost count of how many books she had read that year. The local librarians and the bus driver knew her well. Her mother had home-schooled her, and together they made it through until Abby had received a scholarship to boarding school in Truro. This sadly had left her mother alone on the moor in the draughty old cottage.

Abigail could see her mother standing in the doorway, wrapped in an oversized cardigan from the charity shop. It was far too big, but it had been in the fifty pence bin, so her mother hadn't thought twice. She needed anything that might keep her warm when the wind whipped across the moors, hitting the cottage. It slipped through the gaps in the windows until the fire flickered and what heat there was disappeared up the chimney.

All their meagre funds went to fighting the will. This had been Aunt Teresa's plan. She knew how broke they were and she desired the house and all that went with it. She wanted them to come to her begging. But her mother was too proud, and so was Abby. She would make it without her aunt and without what was rightfully hers.

Abby's father hadn't expected to die at forty-five. Her mother had mentioned that they had spoken about getting a will, but they had always put it off. This had given Teresa the trump card. Teresa knew she would win. She had what Mum and Abby didn't have: money.

Abigail looked at her younger self, feeling all awkward in clothes that were too tatty and small, but she'd refused her sister's hand-me-downs. It hadn't seemed right, and it would have made her mother feel worse than she already did. Her mother walked up to the young Abby and brushed the hair out of her eyes. Chilblains were obvious on her hands. They were raw from washing their clothes by hand. The cottage was so basic, but it had been free.

'My lovely girl, what are you reading?'

'*A Christmas Carol.*'

Her mother shivered and looked out of the window. 'You can imagine it, living here.'

'Yes, especially when the lights flicker and the floors creak.' Abby put the book down and stood. She wrapped her arms around her mother. 'It looks like snow.'

'It does, and here comes the postman. Let's hope he has only good news for us.' She smiled, but it didn't reach her eyes.

Abigail had always thought her mother believed there genuinely would be good news, but viewing the scene now with youth behind her, she saw that her mother had put on the act for her. It was the loneliest Christmas, as Jaks hadn't come home to them. Behind her mother was a bucket they had filled with beautiful driftwood. They had walked the beaches of the north coast and collected shells to decorate the wood. All her mother's decorations were in Scorrier House and Teresa hadn't let her have anything, even those ornaments that had never belonged to the Scorrier side of the family. The delicate glass ornaments had belonged to Abby's maternal great-grandmother. Abigail knew losing her own family heirlooms had broken her mother's heart more than losing the house that had been their home so briefly. She had often said that if they had inherited Scorrier House, she would have sold it and bought a small place by the sea. Where she and Abby could have walked the beach daily and spent each night in front of a roaring fire drinking hot chocolate.

The cottage had smelled wonderful, though. A small pot of water with cloves and a cinnamon stick hung above the fire. It filled the small room with a lovely fragrance even if they didn't have Christmas cakes or mince pies. Her mother was good at making the most of whatever they had. She never showed Abby how much it brought her down, but Abby remembered the muffled sobs she heard late at night when her mother thought she was sleeping. Abigail walked towards her mother and longed to take her into her arms. She should have hugged her more.

The ghost led her away, and they flew over the clay mountains of St Austell until they reached Truro, where Abby was on the school hockey pitch. The teams were tied until she scored the winning goal. Her teammates lifted her off the ground and carried her to the side of the pitch, triumphant. Even now she could feel the thrill of being part of something and helping them reach their victory. At seventeen, she had never been so happy, for she had everything at her feet. The joy and freedom of being in the Upper Sixth, as well as sitting on an offer from Oxford to study English Literature. She had good friends and a boyfriend, Max. He was already at Oxford but would be home in Cornwall for Christmas. She didn't have long to wait, as he broke for the holidays in a few days.

The ghost moved her to the changing room. Abigail knew what was coming. Her chest tightened. It was so unfair. The headmaster of the school stood waiting for her while the smells of sweat and shampoo vied with each other as they drifted out the doorway. Steam from the showers coated the walls and the nearby lockers. Abigail ground her teeth as she watched her seventeen-year-old self, standing buoyant from the win but worried by the headmaster's frown.

'Abby, can you come with me.' His face was so solemn, but then it would be with the devastating blow he had to deliver.

Abby turned to her friends heading into the showers and shrugged. 'Sure, sir.' The ghost and Abigail followed the pair through the grounds to the headmaster's office. Her younger self had no idea what was to come. She had expected that there was a problem with money. That had happened before. They stood inside his office facing each other. 'Abby, I'm afraid I have some terrible news.'

Emotions played across Abby's face. Abigail remembered what she had been thinking. It had to be about Jaks, because he had never looked so serious when there was a problem with money. Reckless Jaks was always in trouble, but she had calmed down since she'd given birth to Freddie last year. Abby's face lost all colour. The headmaster wouldn't be telling her Jaks was in jail again for minor drug offences, that was in the past. Jaks now had Freddie, and she had changed. Besides, that was her mother's task. No, Abby knew then that it was about Mum.

'Sir?' She swallowed.

'I'm afraid I've had a call from Derriford Hospital. Abby, I'm very sorry to tell you that your mother has died.'

'No.' The young Abby stood motionless as her bright world turned dark. It couldn't be so. It couldn't. She held in the scream, waiting to burst forth.

'Your mother had stopped to give a beggar a pound, and she was hit by a car that slid on the icy road.' He spoke slowly, as if he understood that Abby was struggling to take in his words. 'She hit her head when she fell to the ground.' He put a hand on her arm, but Abby pulled away.

'No.' It sounded more like a cry than a word. Abigail knew

as she watched the solemn teenager that everything inside was shattering into a million pieces.

'I'll take you to Matron.'

Abby's face was ashen, and even now standing outside the school Abigail could feel the pain in her chest. Her heart had been ripped out that day. Yet she knew it had been so typical of her mother to give away what they didn't have to give. Her mother had always said that there were people worse off than they were. She felt it had been her duty to help others. All that had done was get her killed, killed for her kindness. Had she ignored the man, the car wouldn't have hit her and it would have hit the beggar instead.

Abigail knew where the ghost would take her next: the funeral. It was a small and dignified affair for which Teresa paid to keep up appearances. Abby had to swallow her pride and let her. She'd had no choice. No matter what, she was determined to bury her mother with her father. The young Abby stood with her back rigid in the front pew of the church, wearing her school uniform, for she had nothing else that was fit for the purpose. Max played the organ and most of the school choir had turned up to sing. That had nearly been her undoing, but she wouldn't let Teresa see her break. Jaks sobbed uncontrollably, reflecting what Abby had wanted to do; but she had to be strong for her mum. Meanwhile, Teresa looked the picture of the grieving relative, dressed in a chic black suit, clutching a lace-trimmed hanky.

Turning to the ghost, she pleaded silently. She didn't want to hear the choir sing or Max play. But the ghost led her down the aisle past the mourners to the choir loft. Max's auburn head was bent over the keys and Abigail clutched her hands together, gripping so hard her nails dug into her skin. Max's hair fell over his eyes and he needed to push the hair away or he wouldn't be able to see the music. Then she released her hands, remembering he didn't need to see this music. He'd composed this piece and called it 'Abby's Grief'. The notes went to minor before soaring into the reaches of the church like a ray of sun bursting from behind a cloud.

'Please take me away.' Abigail tugged on the ghost's cloak.


Despite having the duvet from the train carriage still draped about her shoulders, Abigail was feeling the chill. They walked across the frozen moor and suddenly they were in a pub in Oxford. Max's arm was thrown over Abby's shoulder and they joined in song with the rest of the crowd before breaking off to sing the descant. It was one of Max's compositions that nodded towards his Cornish roots. It was so good. Abby's face was full of pride.

'Let's go carolling,' shouted one friend.

'Then they won't pay to see us in two night's time,' said another.

'Who cares, it's almost Christmas.'

The next thing, they were all bundled up and out on the streets singing to anyone that would listen. Soon people joined them and the small group swelled. They stopped in front of the gates outside the Sheldonian Theatre, arranging themselves on the steps. Even the stragglers seemed to know where they should be.

Max hit the key on the pitch pipe. They all began 'The Holly and the Ivy', breaking out into parts as they set off arm in arm singing until they reached the next pub, Abigail and the ghost following the small crowd growing around the carollers. Christmas trees sparkled from windows and a cheer rose from another group of students across the road, who began 'We Wish You A Merry Christmas'. Even a cabbie pulled up to listen.

When snow began falling, Abby had thought her heart would burst for joy. She and Max were spending Christmas together with his parents. Tomorrow they would set off to Cornwall.

It was well past midnight when they waved goodbye to the others. Max took her by the hand as they walked back to his place. Abby spun around, trying to catch snowflakes on her tongue. As a big flake landed on her nose, she turned to Max and kissed him. 'I love you.'

He pulled her close and whispered in her ear, 'I love you too. I always will.'

Abigail turned from the young couple, remembering his scent and his suddenly serious face. Back then, she had wanted to hold on to the magic of that night. The ghost forced her to watch and her stomach clenched in longing. She had tried so hard to forget this moment.

Abby stroked his cheek and her freezing finger tingled as it stopped at the corner of his mouth. 'Say those words again.' She moved her finger and kissed him. With her lips next to his she whispered, 'You are my heart.'

'No, you are mine.' He pulled away and dropped to his knee. Abby stared, opened mouthed. He took her hand. 'Abigail Scorrier, you are the most beautiful, the most clever and the most wonderful woman ever. Will you marry me?'

Abby looked down on to his face as snowflakes rested in his auburn hair and knew there was no one else she could ever love more. 'Of course I will! But not yet.' She pulled him off the ground.

'Is that a promise?' He looked into her eyes.

'Yes, cross my heart. I will marry you, Max Opie. But let me finish uni and get a job first.'

He held her so tight she thought she'd never breathe again. 'I love you.'

'I hope so, since you asked me to marry you.' She laughed as she stroked his face, loving the splash of freckles across his skin.

Someone above them flung open a window and the sounds of 'Silent Night' drifted out on to the night air.

'Oh, I forgot this.' He took out a small box from his pocket.

Abby's hand flew to her mouth. She had thought Max's proposal was spur of the moment.

'I saw this ring a year ago in an antique shop. It took some convincing for the woman to let me pay for it in instalments, but she did.' He opened the box and there was an art deco diamond and sapphire ring.

'Oh, it's perfect.' The tiny diamonds glittered around the deep blue central sapphire.

Max took her hand and slipped the ring on her finger. 'From the first day I saw you, I have wanted to ask you to marry me.' He raised her hand to his mouth. He turned the palm to his lips and he kissed the base of each finger. 'Don't make me wait too long.'

Abigail opened her fist and looked to where his mouth had lingered. Desire stirred even now.

The ghost took her hand and led her away. 'Max,' she whispered as she wiped a tear from her cheek.


When they flew over the bowling green and Grylls Monument in Helston, Abigail knew what was next. Her chest constricted. She didn't want to see this again. It had been hard enough living through it the first time. Her heart had broken open after seeing Max, but the ghost led her onwards until she stood in the little flat. By the door a picture of Jaks and Freddie sat on the chest of drawers, and near the window a small tree stood decorated with shells and paper garlands. She and Freddie had made them together. Her nephew cuddled on Abby's lap as she read *'Twas the Night Before Christmas*. At six years old, with his dark curls and brown eyes, he was the image of Jaks. Jaks had been gone for two years by then. Years that had altered every one of Abby's plans.

The knock interrupted the story and Abby slipped Freddie off her lap and looked at the bag packed by the door. She didn't understand why he couldn't stay two more days and be with her for Christmas. But no, Aunt Teresa had her way again. She was the one who put social services on her case, saying she was unfit to look after Freddie. She was far fitter than his mother had been, and certainly more so than the mean old woman that was her aunt. No one could see that Teresa only wanted Freddie because he looked like Jaks who, like their grandfather and Freddie, was a Scorrier. That was important to her aunt; which made no sense to Abby, since she too was a Scorrier yet Teresa had never shown her any care or concern. Teresa had all the money and Abby was struggling to pay the bills. Between child-care and rent, there was nothing to spare. This alone seemed to make Teresa the better choice of guardian.

Abby hesitated until a further knock forced her to open the door.

'Merry Christmas,' the woman said with a bright smile plastered across her face.

Abby wanted to shout, *You have a nerve saying that to me*. Instead she said, 'Are you sure that this has to happen now and couldn't wait until after Boxing Day?'

'We've been through this. Having Freddie at your aunt's for Christmas will help him adjust to his new home.'

My home, thought Abby. Everything had gone to Aunt Teresa and now Freddie was going too. Everyone thought Teresa could better look after him. But it was a lie. She was older, yes – sixty-six to Abby's twenty-two – but not wiser. However, social services wouldn't see Abby's side. They said she didn't have the means or the time. She earned so little making films for non-profit organisations. Abby could barely provide for herself, let alone a child. She couldn't argue with that, but she did, nonetheless.

The woman picked up Freddie's bag and held out her hand to the child. Abby had received a promise of a review of the case if her circumstances changed. She needed to earn a lot of money fast. The question was how. Already she had turned down a job with the BBC in Manchester. Not that that would have generated enough money to cover costs, but it would have been a step in the right direction for her career. She had one hope. A friend of a friend had been interested in her CV. He made commercials and music videos.

Abby turned to Freddie, who was waiting on the sofa for her to finish the poem. They had read it every night this week, and now she wouldn't be able to finish. Every Christmas Eve since he'd been born, she'd read it to him.

'Freddie, Mrs Smith is here to take you to Great Aunt Teresa's.'

'OK,' he said, but he pointed to the open page of the book. 'But you haven't finished the story.'

Abby swallowed and looked to Mrs Smith, who pointed to her watch. Time was up.

'I'll read it to you soon.' She took a deep breath. 'Take it with you.'

Freddie closed the book and picked up his stuffed rabbit. He looked at her with eyes wide open, not understanding why he was going to a sleepover at Great Aunt Teresa's house. Abby fell to her knees and held open her arms. Freddie, clutching Rabbit and the book, came to her. 'I love you, Abby.'

'I love you too.'

'Time to go, Freddie. Give your aunt a kiss and then put your coat on.'

Freddie planted a sloppy wet kiss on Abby's cheek and she closed her eyes. She couldn't do this.

'Happy Christmas, Abby. Will Father Christmas find me at Great Aunt Teresa's?'

Abby nodded, unable to speak. She kissed him on the head and breathed in his scent. Somehow she would find the money and find it fast so she could keep the promise she'd made to Jaks all those years ago. This was so wrong.

Abigail turned to the spirit with tears pooling in her eyes. 'No more, please.' He pointed to Freddie heading out of the door, trailing Rabbit behind him. Her younger self blew kisses to her nephew, which he pretended to catch and then hold to his heart.


The snow had accumulated on the moor, but Abby couldn't see their footsteps as they walked towards the Tor, which strangely morphed into Bristol. Abby was an assistant director for a small production company. She had begun to earn decent money. Three years had passed since that Christmas Eve when Freddie had been taken from her.

The clock on the wall of the editing desk showed it was ten-thirty. Seven hours ago everyone had left the building to head home and begin the celebrations, but Abby sat alone in the near dark, running through the week's rushes. Something had been lost in the editing and they were on a tight deadline. The story didn't carry the emotional punch it needed, and this production would be her calling card. It needed to be perfect, and it needed to be done by the twenty-eighth. No one else cared. It was Christmas, so they had ticked the boxes. She didn't work that way. Nothing was as important as landing the next job, which would mean more money and another step closer to getting Freddie back.

Her phone beeped. Max's name flashed up on the screen.

'Shit.' She was supposed to have been on the seven o'clock train to Truro. Her bag was by her feet.

She pressed the green button. 'Sorry.'

'Are you OK?'

'Yes, I'm editing, or more correctly fixing the editing.'

'It's Christmas Eve.'

'It doesn't matter. I'll drive down tomorrow.' She turned to the screen and began searching for what had been cut again.

'Did you hear what I said?'

'Sorry, no.'

'I saw Freddie.'

Abby closed her eyes. This was why she was doing this. 'How was he?'

'He's grown and he has a fine voice.'

'How do you know?' She fiddled with a knob, adjusting the focus.

'He was singing with his school choir at the cathedral tonight.'

Abby sucked in air then asked, 'Was she there?'

'No.' Max sighed. 'He was the only one without family in the audience.'

'I didn't know.'

'Would you have come if you had?' She could hear his frustration.

'Of course.' But as she said the words and saw the missing shots on the screen, she knew she lied.

'I love you, Abby.'

'I love you too.' She was focused on beginning the process of re-editing. 'See you tomorrow.' She pressed the red button, cutting Max off as he spoke.

As the ghost swept her away, she recalled she hadn't driven to Cornwall on Christmas Day but had worked straight through.

The wind whipped the small flakes about and she shivered as they left Bristol and appeared on the rainswept streets of

Chelsea. Abby stopped walking. She didn't want to see this Christmas, but the ghost wasn't giving her any choice. They walked past the decorated storefronts until they reached a small Italian restaurant. Inside she could see herself and Max sitting with a half-empty bottle of water between them. It was Christmas Eve, and he was about to drive to Cornwall. Abby had a gin and tonic in front of her.

'Come with me. You need a break.' He reached out for her hands. Her engagement ring reflected the glow of the fairy lights.

'Can't. I need to be in London first thing on Boxing Day for filming.'

'Who else will be there?' He traced his fingers over hers, sending messages to her body that her brain didn't want to receive.

'No one. We begin the following day. There is so much that has to be done and it will cost a small fortune if we delay.'

'So you are doing this on your own?' His beautiful hazel eyes were wary but pleading with her to see reason.

'Yes.' Abby looked at their reflection in the glass and, squinting, she could make out the last-minute shoppers moving through the afternoon gloom.

'Why?'

Abby turned to him with a sigh. They had been through this before. 'Because I need to get ahead.'

Max shook his head. 'You were never like this before.'

Abby took a sip of her drink, thinking she had been like this for a while. He didn't understand. 'I need to make a decent living so I can get Freddie back.'

'You know that won't happen now. It's been too long.'

'No.' Abby shook her head even though she half believed him. It had been seven years since Teresa had taken Freddie from her. He was nearly thirteen and in those six years she'd

47

been allowed to see him once a year and always supervised, as if she was a criminal and not his aunt.

Abby played with her engagement ring and Max took her hand in his again. 'I know you want the best for him and have tried to earn enough to have him back. But it isn't going to happen. Your aunt is too well connected and has too much money.'

She looked at Max's fingers stroking hers. They were musician's hands, long and elegant. He made very little money, but he created beautiful music. Music had brought them together in the first place, in the school choir, but now Abby couldn't remember the last time she had sung, not even in the shower. Music had left her life.

'I've been offered a job at a prep school in Cambridge. Give up this ridiculous quest and do what you promised to do all those years ago.' His fingers touched her hand while his glance pleaded with her. Her heart leapt at the thought.

Abigail turned to the ghost. She couldn't watch what comes next.

'Let's have our own family and maybe Freddie will be allowed to come and visit.'

Abby's eyes opened wide and she saw all the love shining out of Max's. He really thought it would work and that it would be enough. Even after he had said that it was Teresa's money that was blinding everyone to the reality that Freddie was in boarding school and lonely. Freddie's letters to her broke her heart. All she could do was tell him he was loved and that his mother had loved him so much. Despite pleading with Teresa, she couldn't get custody. It always came back to the fact that she couldn't provide for him as well as her aunt. She had to do what she had to do – make more money. And she was almost there. One more move up and she would be more than an associate. Abby would be the director and the money would come. She had to do this, for she had promised.

Abby brought his hand to her mouth and kissed it, then placed it gently on the table. With shaky fingers, she wiggled the engagement ring off. It was holding them both back. If she walked away, Max could pursue his compositions, not teach kids to sing; while she would break through and earn enough to provide for Freddie.

Her decision was made. She should have done this years ago. It was the only fair thing to do. Set him free. She handed the ring to him.

'Don't do this.' His eyes filled, but the tears didn't fall. 'Don't.'

Abby stood and turned away. She dropped some money on the table and walked out of the restaurant. Not looking back, afraid of what she would see, afraid of what she would do.

But now, all these years later, Abigail looked at Max's face with the courage she hadn't had then. He sat there turning over the ring in his fingers as if that would make her come back. She couldn't. He deserved to find someone who would love him as much as he had loved her. Her heart stopped as the memories of that love filled her. Could she bear knowing that he gave any of that love to someone else? Blocking him and his love from her mind was the only way she had been able to move forward. By denying his existence she survived, but right now there he was, beautiful and broken, and she had done the last part. She had taken his loving heart and walked all over it. Had it been only to make enough money for Freddie? Or had it been that she needed to succeed to prove Teresa wrong? The woman had said she would never make anything of herself. She had said that she was as weak as Jaks and as foolish as her mother. Abby had been determined to prove her wrong, and now the woman was dead. What had it all been for? Freddie.

· · ·

49

Abigail pulled the duvet closer around her as she looked again through the restaurant window. Max sat with his head in his hands. That was the last time she had seen him. And she had been so wrong. It hadn't been only for Freddie; she had become hooked on success and power. She had thrown his love away.

The ghost led them on and Abigail recognised the granite building on Lemon Street, Truro. This was her last visit to Cornwall.

Abby stood in the solicitor's office looking out of the window at heavy rain. Beside the big desk, Teresa sat with her ankles delicately crossed, watching as the lawyer pushed the paper-work across the desk.

'I shouldn't have to do this. This is not what Jaks wanted. She wanted me in Freddie's life.'

'You've upset his life, interfered with his schooling. This is for the best.' She pushed the papers towards Abby. Abby paced, kicking herself for calling the school; but she had been worried about Freddie. That had set off a chain of events that led to this moment. It was blackmail, but no one but her would call it that.

'Miss Scorrier, if you sign the document stating that you will only contact Freddie twice a year – Christmas and his birthday, in writing – then your aunt has agreed that Scorrier House and her wealth will go to him.' He held out the pen.

Abby's mouth dried, longing to talk to Max, but she'd cast him out of her life and she was alone. This was the last thing that she wanted. She'd promised Jaks she would look after Freddie, but she'd lost her job. She signed.

Shivering, Abigail stood beside the ghost. In front of them was Max, alone at the piano working out a tune. Abigail heard the sea in the beat and saw the sadness etched in the lines beside his mouth. The melancholy of the notes tore at her heart.

'Tell me when this is.' Abigail looked around the room for some indication of the date. The ghost pointed to the newspaper on the piano. There was a picture of her with an actor at a premiere in London. 2010. She remembered it well; the film, that was. The actor was nothing, but the picture told a different story. Abigail watched as Max put the pencil down and played. Loud, harsh, discordant.

The ghost held out his hand and Abigail took one last look at Max, knowing what he was thinking. But it was wrong. The actor was not her lover and never had been.

The ghost set them down outside a small building tucked among pines on the side of a river. Music floated out. They were in Cornwall again, but she wasn't sure where.

'Max, I love what you've done with the addition of these chords running through,' said a woman. Abigail dragged her feet as the ghost led them through the door. She could tell by the admiring tone in the voice that she didn't want to see this.

Max was grinning as he looked up at the owner of the voice. Abigail's heart stopped. She'd seen that look of love before.

'It's thanks to you and your brilliant insight.' He slid over on the piano stool. 'Can you sing through this bit here?' He touched the sheet music and the woman leaned closer to Max. Her red hair glistened in the light as it fell on to his shoulder.

'Yes.'

The woman nodded and pulled her torso up while she cleared her throat. Max played a note then her voice filled the space. Abigail's chest tightened. Words of love so beautiful surrounded them. Max wrote them and this woman was singing them back to him.

Abigail walked out of the door. Max had found love again. She couldn't bear to see. 'Please, take me away.'

# Stave Three

## The Second of the Three Spirits

Abigail rolled over when she heard a snore, then realised it wasn't the man in the cabin next door. It was her. She sat up in bed. The train was gently swaying. They must not be on the moor any longer. A glance at her watch showed one o'clock. But of course, it was one o'clock again. Why would she think it was anything else? She was caught in a nightmare, or the train was moving through a time warp of some sort. Frequently it had felt that way when she had travelled back over the Tamar. A land lost in time – that was Cornwall through and through. But this was different and couldn't be real.

But if Jaks was correct, there should be a second ghost. A second ghost. Abigail had lost her mind. She looked around the small cabin. Where was he, she, it? Abigail glanced at the window, but the shade was firmly shut. She tapped the crystal of her watch. Five past the hour and there was no ghost. She pulled her knees to her chest and waited. Another ten minutes passed. She bit the side of her nail, then stopped. She hadn't done that in ages.

Clutching her duvet, she stood and headed to the window, ready to open the blind, when she saw a light glowing under the door. Her hand on the lever, she hesitated. This was madness, but something compelled her. Was it the memory of Jaks' face? She pushed the handle down and pulled the door open.

'Come in,' a deep voice called. It certainly wasn't the voice of the train guard, unless she had changed sex. Abigail stumbled into the narrow corridor that ran along the cabin. She was sure it was the corridor, but it didn't look like it had done earlier. It was taller and wider and decorated with richly fragrant boughs of pine and holly. Where the carriage joined the next, there was a tall Christmas tree festooned with candles, baubles and topped with an angel covered in gossamer threads that reflected the light. Abby pinched her thigh to make sure she wasn't still tucked under the duvet on the narrow berth, dreaming. The train halted sharply, and she reached out to steady herself as her glance fell on a tall man leaning casually against one of the windows. 'Good evening. Come closer.'

Abby nodded. He was hard to miss. The light around him moved like he had a disco ball on his person somewhere.

'I am the Ghost of Christmas Present.' He was dressed in a richly embroidered dressing gown that looked like it had been stolen off a mannequin in Shanghai Tang's. It gaped at the top, revealing a muscled, hairy chest. She dared to glance lower and saw that he wore black satin pyjama bottoms with his feet bare. In his large hand he held a magnum of Bollinger and two champagne flutes. His hair was wild, as if he'd already been partying for hours, and he wore a ridiculous gold paper crown from a Christmas cracker at a rakish angle.

'I could tell. You look like you've been at the party for a while.'

'I have and a good one it is. Have you met my brothers?'

She frowned, thinking of the party animals she'd met over the years. But none resembled him. 'Not that I know of. Is it important?' She blinked, wondering if he meant the Ghost of Christmas Past.

He frowned, then stood straight.

'I don't know what you have planned for me, but take me. I'm ready.' Abigail glanced up at the ghost, wondering if she really was. So far tonight, if it was tonight, she had seen some of her happiest and most painful memories. All of them had been buried deep within her so that she hadn't let herself think about them for years. Only in dreams did they appear. What would this ghost show her? Could it be any worse?

'Grab hold of my robe and we shall be off.'

The railway carriage melted away, and she held on for dear life. They flew over frosted fields and across the sea with the waves rolling below. Soon she recognised the gaslights of Beacon Hill in Boston as they touched down in the Public Garden next to the brass ducklings. They were decorated for the holiday and dusted in snow. She had been so surprised to see this odd arrangement of statues here when she had first arrived in Boston three years ago. But shortly after, they had made a short film about the children's book *Make Way For The Ducklings* and the place it held in the hearts of Bostonians.

The ghost led them through the snow-covered streets of Beacon Hill until they came to the Church of the Advent on Brimmer Street. The sounds of a choir practising 'Good King Wenceslas' could be heard. She swallowed. She'd always loved that carol. A tramp was repairing his cardboard home as Sophie waddled up to him with a steaming cup of coffee and croissant filled with bacon. She also carried a huge down-filled coat from one of the expensive outdoor shops. She gave it to the tramp. Sophie didn't have that type of money. She earned a pittance. But Abigail watched as her pregnant assistant squatted down and chatted to the bum whom Abby had walked past every day and deliberately crossed the street to avoid. Sophie could be mugged. Someone could walk by and push her over. So many things could go wrong. Yet as Abigail stood there listening, she heard Sophie invite the tramp to join them for Christmas dinner.

'Pete, there's more snow forecast for later today, so why don't you come and join us for dinner?'

'That's very kind, but I'll lose my spot if I go.'

'I'm sure the shelter would take you in tonight of all nights.'

'Bless you.' He said as he stood and put the new coat over the threadbare one he wore.

'That looks much warmer.' Sophie smoothed the fabric over his shoulders.

'It is, it is. You have a heart of gold.'

'Nonsense. It's Christmas, and the joy is in giving.' Sophie beamed at him, but then squealed in pain and clutched her bump. The ghost moved them on, but Abigail was worried at the way Sophie had gone totally white. Would the tramp help her or simply steal her mobile?

The ghost took them away until they stood in front of Abigail's apartment. She could see Ginge in the window where he watched the world go by. There were no decorations adorning her window, unlike every other door and window on the street. Snowflakes drifted past the panes, and Ginge had his nose pressed to the glass. He wouldn't even get a turkey leg this year; only the shrimp, if Becky did as she promised.

As if on cue, Becky walked up the street wrapped in a bright red scarf, clutching a shopping bag. She clearly hadn't forgotten her duty. Ginge leapt down from the window and Abigail could hear him meowing at the door. They followed Becky as she let herself in and bent down to scoop up Ginge. His eyes closed as she scratched under his chin.

'Merry Christmas, Ginge.' The cat stuck his nose in the bag. It must contain the prawns, the passion of his existence.

'Yes, there's a treat in there for you.' She put him down on the counter and stroked him from head to tail. 'Life must be simple for a cat.' She paused. 'Well, maybe not for you. You have to put up with her, Miss Grump.' Becky looked around, her glance pausing on the large television. 'She has all the money in the world but not one iota of happiness.' She sighed while Ginge rubbed his head against her hand. 'We may be broke, but at least my family have each other.' She leaned down and kissed Ginge's head. She pulled out a cat bowl and dropped five big fat prawns into the bowl. 'I could have bought a small turkey for the family with what I paid for these things. You, Ginge, you are the only one she treats with respect. I don't think she even sees the people around her. They are just things that help her life or hinder it.'

Becky turned on the television. *It's A Wonderful Life* filled the screen. 'I love this film, Ginge. Is it your favourite too?'

The cat looked up from his feast, purred, and resumed eating it.

Ginge meowed and walked to the sink, where Becky turned on the tap for him to drink. Abby wanted to point out he had a mechanised watering bowl for this purpose that didn't waste water. But she stopped as she heard Becky talking again to Ginge.

'If I had three wishes this Christmas, I would wish for Sam and Jane to find an apartment that they could afford so they could build their own family without everyone watching every move they made. I would want the money to pay for Mom to have her hip replaced and –' Becky paused as she turned off the tap '– I wish that Abigail Scorrier would find her heart. I'm sure she must have had one once, otherwise she wouldn't love you so much, Ginge.' He sidled up to her, rubbing his head against her arms before he jumped down and settled on the sofa, watching the film.

'I can't stay right now. I'm off to church to help.' She rubbed his head and he purred. 'I'll leave this on for you and I'll come back when I've finished.' He meowed. 'Don't worry. She'll never know I left the television on.' He replied by rubbing his head

56

against her hand. 'The electricity won't be that much. See you later.'

Abigail looked at Ginge cleaning himself, keeping half an eye on the television screen. Was she that much of a miser that she would complain about the television being left on? She closed her eyes, knowing the answer.

The ghost brought them away from her unadorned door and they arrived at Massachusetts General Hospital, where the tramp sat with Sophie's husband, Tim, in a waiting room. Both men sat close together, clutching cups and jumping at the sound of every passing footstep.

'Thank God you were with her, Pete.'

'It was nothing. In fact, it was down to the cell phone she'd given me in the summer. It meant I could call for help, and call you, of course.'

'Do you think she'll be OK?' Tim stood and began pacing the room.

'I wish I knew.'

Abigail looked anxiously to the ghost as he poured some champagne in their plastic cups and then took them on to a church hall. Christmas carols were being pounded out on an old upright piano while the vicar, in a Santa hat, greeted the homeless as they made their way into the warmth of the hall. Becky was wearing an elf hat at a rakish angle and laughing as she handed out the last plate, fully loaded with Christmas dinner and all the trimmings.

She turned to the woman next to her. 'Right, I've gotta dash. I have a date with a poor boy who has been left all on his own tonight.'

'Have fun,' the vicar called from the piano.

'Merry Christmas all.' Becky raced out of the hall and up the hill towards Abigail's apartment. The ghost followed her, having filled every glass in the place with his never-empty bottle of bubbly.

Becky slowed down as she reached the apartment, and Abigail saw Tim and the tramp walk past her down the hill. They both looked desolate.

'It's her boss's fault.' Tim shook his head. 'Her doctor said she should be on bed rest, but the bitch said she had to work.' The tramp put his arm around Tim and they walked on.

Abigail looked to the ghost. Sophie was OK, wasn't she?


It was a village that Abby didn't recognise, yet the granite bell tower looked as so many Cornish churches did. The bells were ringing, announcing that the service was about to start. The night was dark and cold. She blinked. There were no services on the evening of Christmas Day. Had they gone back in time? Why was she questioning this when she was flying around with ghosts? Surely that was what she should be worried about. That and her sanity.

A few latecomers dashed up the footpath, giggling. Abigail guessed they had been in the pub. She and the ghost slipped into the packed church behind them. The ringers were emerging as Abigail and the ghost moved up towards the organ in the south transept. The first notes of 'O Come All Ye Faithful' rose from the organ and her heart stopped. Max. He was playing. Although concentrating, his eyes were smiling. She knew because lines that had only appeared when she had last seen him were now etched more clearly. The beautiful red-haired woman stood at his side along with a blonde teenager. So what Abigail had seen with the Ghost of Christmas Past had been true. As the woman flipped the sheet of music, he smiled at her. Abigail remembered that smile. A hole opened inside.

She turned to leave, but the ghost held his hand up, stopping her. She looked away from Max, unable to watch him. It was clear he was happy. For that she was grateful, but she didn't want to see him with another woman. Yet she knew she needed to, for she had been the one to walk away, not him. It was right that he had moved on. The woman was probably the reason he was here in this church and not with his parents in St Austell.

The vicar welcomed everyone, but Abigail didn't listen to the words of this first service of Christmas. There was some shuffling, then the woman and the teen grouped together along with a small choir. Silence filled the church. A voice so pure swirled around the ancient building. Abigail gasped. 'Once in Royal David's City'. It was the soprano. No wonder Max was in love. Who wouldn't fall for that voice?

She tried again to leave and still the ghost wouldn't let her. As the hymn finished, she saw Max's eyes shine with happiness and pride. Abigail could watch no more.


Abigail took the ghost's hand, wondering where they were heading now. The north coast of Cornwall appeared in front of her. If this was the Ghost of Christmas Present, why was he hovering over the beaches of her past?

The sun hung lower above the horizon, casting a twinkling light across the frost-encrusted cliffs. Below the rocks, on a wide sweep of golden sand, were a crowd of mad people about to take a Christmas Day swim. They landed next to a woman holding a steaming thermos scented with cloves. An elderly man clutched an old-fashioned bellyboard like one her father had had. He'd always claimed he had no time for modern ones when the old ones worked as well.

The waves broke further out, sending in gentler rollers that ran up the beach. Sunlight slanted through a disappearing mist, giving everything a soft focus. The morning was beautiful as Abby looked around. Plumes of fogged breath came from everyone's mouths.

'Happy Christmas, all. Remember, it has to be a full immersion up to the neck to count. If you all manage it, the total raised for the neonatal unit will be two thousand pounds.' The vicar paused. 'Remember, in today's world we don't need any children in a stable.' She then removed her dog collar and quickly revealed a sensible black one-piece. Abby sighed with relief. She recalled a vicar doing the swim in her childhood who wore speedos. She was not sure she had ever recovered.

A well wrapped-up man began a countdown and when he had finally reached one, the crowd of thirty raced into the water. Abby remembered the thrill. She could almost see her goose bumps now as she and Max had held hands and run into the waves. She swallowed hard.

Turning to the ghost. 'Take me on, please.' He nodded, and she grabbed his robe as all the swimmers had reached their necks. The elderly man with the bellyboard caught a wave and cruised up the beach. As they flew above Abigail saw the hot mulled wine being served to the adults as they huddled in big towels.

The sun was high in the sky and it was painfully blue. Abigail had forgotten it could be like that. Why had she only remembered the rain and the wind? They flew over her old family home, Scorrier House. The bright light reflected off the tall Georgian windows. Her aunt lay dead in there, or maybe in a nearby funeral home. Surely the ghost would not take her to see the woman who had single-handedly ruined her life. Even on this glorious Christmas Day, Abigail couldn't find it in herself to forgive the woman. Maybe there was no hope for Abigail if she couldn't find forgiveness. Her aunt had stolen everything from them, from her.

They soared over the garden, which looked beautiful still encrusted with frost. Where was Freddie? She should be with him, helping him to deal with all of this. Knowing her aunt, she wouldn't have left the house to Freddie but to a local dog's charity or something else, out of spite. Abigail noticed the loose slates on the roof. And the disarray of the flower beds beyond the immediate surroundings of the house. In fact, as the noonday sun rose to its peak, she noticed how shabby the place looked. What had her aunt done?

Before she could assess the place any further, they came down in the village near the pub. People were heading into it, calling out greetings to each other. Children clutched their new toys and adults winked to each other over the kids' heads as people asked what Father Christmas had brought them. Abby remembered the joy on Christmas morning when she found her stocking and would run to Jaks' room to collect her before heading into her parents' room. She would climb on to their big bed and slowly open all her gifts. Hers was always filled with books, and Jaks' had always contained a doll of some sort.

The ghost directed her into the pub. It was smoke-free and so different to her memories of it. The paint was bright and decorations tasteful. Ivy twisted around the beams with bright red ribbons securing it all.

'So sorry about your Great Aunt Teresa. Rotten time of year to deal with death.'

Abigail turned from the decor and looked at Freddie. Plump cheeks had been replaced with hollows and a neat beard. She searched for the child and saw only a young man. So much time had passed and she'd missed it all.

Freddie clutched his pint and nodded. Abigail didn't recognise any of the other people in the pub. But Freddie did, judging by the people milling about him and offering words of condolence.

'You must come join us for dinner. Can't have you all alone in the big house with a tin of baked beans.' A tall woman placed a hand on his arm.

'Thanks, Millie, I think I might take you up on that.'

'Do. Christmas is no time to be on your own.'

He nodded and Abby turned away. Where had the little boy who'd snuggled in her arms listening to *'Twas the Night before Christmas* gone? Standing at the bar, Freddie was a man now, near enough. He was tall and looked a bit like she remembered her father looking. Jaks would be proud of him.

'What has become of your aunt? Abby, wasn't it?'

Freddie looked into his pint. 'She's in television, she is, in the States.'

'Too stuck-up for us lot now, I bet, but once upon a time she used to be here singing away with her dad.' The man laughed. 'Now he was a good man.' He shook his head. 'Shame his daughters turn out so bad.'

Freddie coughed.

'Sorry, lad. You turned out all right enough.'

Someone began singing, and Abigail wanted to linger longer as she saw Freddie join in the rounds. She remembered them so well. Without thinking, she had begun to raise her voice in tune with the women's round when the ghost beckoned her away. They travelled across Cornwall, stopping briefly at the cathedral in Truro to see the people filing in for a service. They swept past and continued on until they came to a river and there sitting above it was a great house. It must be nearly four o'clock, the daylight was fading and water below was a dark grey. From the large windows of the house, white candles gleamed. On the corner of the house facing the river, she spotted a tall Christmas tree covered in small white lights and red and silver ornaments. Lametta tinsel dripped from the boughs. It was what she always thought a tree should look like, elegant and regal, perfect for its surrounding in this house. The last Christmas at Scorrier House they had had a tree like this. Abigail swallowed.

The ghost drew them closer to the house and she could hear a piano playing. It was the Cornish curl version of 'While Shepherds Watched their Flocks by Night'. She and the ghost drifted through the window and he went about to twenty people around the piano, topping up the champagne glasses without them noticing.

'For those of you not from Cornwall, you won't know this version, but we prefer it.' It was Max speaking. 'It is sung in rounds known as curls. So, Mark and Tristan, I'm relying on you to lead the men; and Hannah and Gabe, you know the score for the women.' He played a few notes, then stopped. 'Why don't we show them how it's done on the first verse, then begin again.'

The red-haired singer was there at Max's side. Abigail swallowed, but her mouth remained dry.

Max began playing the hymn. 'All sing.'
*While Shepherds watched their flocks by night*
*All seated on the ground*
*The Angel of the Lord came down*
'Now, men only . . . *And glory shone around.*' Max looked to Hannah and Gabe. 'Now the woman jump in.'
*And glory shone around.*

'Let's all give it a try. It might help if you divide yourselves.' He grinned as the party shifted position around the piano.

Abigail was shaking. Here was Max again and he sounded happy. The music moved around her. She was pleased, she really was. The presence of the beautiful woman confirmed her suspicions. She was his partner now. He deserved happiness. A tear slipped down Abigail's cheek as she moved closer to join them on the chorus. These words were stamped into her soul.

When the song finished, she saw the ghost adding more champagne to the punch on the sideboard. She glanced at Max. His eyes. How she loved those eyes. He looked at her, but she knew he couldn't see her. What had she given up? He bent his head to the keyboard again and began the next carol.

. . .

Outside Truro's Hall for Cornwall, Abby looked at the crowds entering. Emblazoned on the posters was Max's name and there was a picture of the singer looking windswept, her eyes full of longing. *The Lovers.*

'No,' Abigail said, not budging, but the ghost put a hand to her back. They went through the stage door. The heat of the lights and the smell of greasepaint filled the air. She took small steps as the ghost manoeuvred her to the edge of the stage where she could see Max in the pit directing the orchestra, while on stage there was an old crone perched on a rock watching the soprano below her. The soprano began singing.

*I am thine,*
*Thou art mine,*
*Beyond control,*

A trap door opened on the stage and tenor's voice joined the soprano's.

*In the wave*
*Be the grave*
*Of heart and soul . . . of heart and soul*

The soprano walked towards him.

They both disappeared from the stage and the old crone came running down to save them, but they were gone.

The curtain came down, and the audience were on their feet. The cast came out and took the first call and so it went on until the beautiful woman pulled Max on to the stage, where he took a bow. Then she kissed him. Abigail could look no longer. With or without the ghost, she could not watch. As she moved through the crowds, she heard the chatter.

'What a triumph.'

'So much heart. And didn't Gabriella Blythe shine tonight? Cornwall will not be able to hold her.'

'Or him.'

'Sheer brilliance to use the legend of the lovers of Porthgwarra.'

'Genius, and what a muse to inspire him.'

'Please, take me away. I'm happy for Max, but I can bear to watch any longer.'

# Stave Four

## The Last of the Spirits

Abigail's cheeks were wet, and the train rocked with a gentle motion. She was back in the bunk. Wrapping her arms tight around her body, she curled into the foetal position while she waited for the third ghost. Would this be the Ghost of Christmas Future? Had what she'd seen already happened? She had lost all sense of time and even of place. She looked to the window and there stood a phantom, not a ghost. Gone was the jolly glow of Christmas Present. In front of her was a hooded, robed figure. It towered over her and, despite looking up to it, she could see no face. It was lost in the shadows. She shivered. This was not a promising start. She missed the Ghost of Christmas Present and his bottle of happiness.

'Are you the Ghost of Christmas Future?'

There was a slight dip of the hooded head. She longed to look at the face but feared it at the same time. Had she ever thought looking into the future would be a good idea? She didn't need help to see her future. She already knew she would be alone.

'Lead on. I am as ready as I will ever be.' Her skin crawled. And they suddenly were back in Boston. Ginge sat in the window, but the curtains were gone. She frowned. Out on the sidewalk stood her neighbours. 'Yes, the cleaner found her this morning but they are not sure when, you know . . .'

The phantom moved on a few streets and into Abigail's office block. They swiftly ascended the stairs to the fifth floor and stood in front of her office. But her name wasn't on the door. A rectangular patch of paler wood gleamed in the winter daylight coming in through the office windows. Why wasn't her name on the door? Had she been promoted and moved to the floor above?

The phantom pointed a bony finger and Abby reluctantly went through the door to see Sophie and Trevor chatting.

'Yes, there's no problem. The filming will go ahead on time; and thank you for your belief that I can do the job.'

'You may not have her balls, but I have every faith that the softer approach will be as effective, if not more so.'

Abigail's shoulders rose as she listened to Trevor speak of her that way. Then her glance fell to Sophie's stomach.

'Tell me, Ghost of Christmas Future, where is Sophie's child?'

He didn't respond, but moved to the stairs and took them through the twilight to the streets of Back Bay. Snow was still falling as they stood outside a second-hand clothes store. She couldn't be sure, but it looked like her Diane von Furstenberg dress hanging on the mannequin in the window. The spirit indicated that they should enter.

'I want all of these things put on consignment. She may have been cheap as hell with everyone, but she didn't stint on her clothes.'

The woman's voice sounded familiar. Abigail squinted in the low light at the back of the shop. By the slight stoop of the shoulders it looked like an older woman, but the voice was young and laced with a heavy Boston accent. Another woman came out of the back room.

'Where did you get these things?'

'Ah, well, you see, the owner didn't need them any longer, and it appears there's no one who cares.'

'Fair enough. It's good stuff so they will sell quickly.'

Abigail looked at the shoes and the handbags on the table. She recognised them all.

'Spirit, tell me, what does this mean?'

He pointed out of the door and with a heavy heart she followed, trying not to piece everything together, for she didn't like the answer. She looked up and they were standing outside her bedroom. She could hear Ginge howling at the window. The door opened and her room was bare, even more so than the usual minimalist appearance. Her closet doors gaped open, revealing very little. Her cleaner had left little. She tried to prepare herself to look at the bed, expecting a bare mattress. But she saw a sheet covering what appeared to be a body. Her skin cooled and goose bumps appeared on her arms.

'Tell me it's not what I think. Please tell me I can change this.'

The phantom didn't move, but pointed for the door.

A soft rain fell and Abby wrapped her arms about herself. The spirit pointed to an old iron gate set in a granite wall. Abby knew where she was. This was where her parents were buried. There was a new grave. The earth had not yet sunk down. She turned to the phantom.

'Please, not this.'

He continued to show that she should walk on. There was a stone above the grave containing the words she didn't want to read.

*Abigail Scorrier*
*1983 to 2017*

It had been her body under the sheet. She had known this even if she hadn't wanted to believe it.

68

'Spirit, please tell me there is time to change this future, that it is . . . is only a shadow of what might be if I don't change . . .'

Abby touched the robe of the phantom and felt her fingers freeze. She released the fabric and dropped to her knees.

'You haven't shown me what has happened to Sophie's child.' She clasped her hands together and when she looked up, they were no longer in Cornwall but in a graveyard in Boston.

*Angela Turner*
*December 25, 2016*

'No, spirit, no. Please, tell me it isn't so?'

His finger remained outstretched towards the grave.

How could she have not seen what her life had become? It all hurt too much. She had worked harder and harder so she would have no time to think. And she had pushed those around her to the edge of their nerves; and look what had happened. Poor Sophie. And how young Becky despised her. How could she ever make this right? She closed her eyes, thinking of Max, and when she opened them again, she was back in her berth.

# Stave Five

## The End of It

The train slowed. Shedding the duvet, she ran to the window, lifting the shade to see dawn was breaking over Mount's Bay. She was supposed to have left the train at Truro, but she could see they were almost in the station at Penzance, the end of the line. Why hadn't the guard woken her?

There was a tap on the door. 'Morning, my lover.'

'Morning.' Abigail opened the door and saw a piece of paper taped to it reading *Change of plan . . . Now getting off at Penzance.* She blinked. Did she write this? The writing looked like hers, but not quite . . . More like Jaks' hand.

The guard stood holding a small tray with her coffee and what smelled like a bacon roll. She was famished. She took the tray with hands that shook.

'Can you tell me what day it is?'

The woman's brows drew together. 'Slept that well, did you? It's Christmas Eve, and a beautiful one it's going to be too.'

'Yes, yes it is. Thank you, and happy Christmas.'

'Thank you, my dear, now have a merry one yourself.'

'Yes, thank you, I think I may.' Abigail gave the woman a swift hug, then closed the door. She picked up the roll and bit into it, letting the salty sweetness fill her mouth. A bacon sarnie had never tasted so good and she washed it down with milky coffee. Heaven. It was seven forty-five as they had reached the platform. She heard the doors of the cabins opening and people calling greetings. It was Christmas Eve, there was still time to make things happen.

The cold, clear smell of chilled sea air filled her lungs as she walked out of the station. It was like she hadn't breathed for years. She could almost taste the sea. A thin layer of frost covered the parked cars, and a mist hung about the water. But the sky was changing from pale blue to cerulean without a cloud to be seen.

The first thing she needed to do was to tell Sophie to take the day off. The office didn't need to be open, and Sophie needed to put her feet up and look after that bump of hers. After she emailed, she looked at the taxi rank and decided she would go straight to Scorrier House and see Freddie. She had bridges to mend and the one to him was the most important.

One of the gate pillars was slightly tilting like it had had too much to drink. She didn't recall it being that way before, but then she hadn't been here in over twenty years. The drive wound through fields until it cut through a small wood, then the house came into view. It stood square and even with its tall windows reflecting the morning sunlight.

'I heard the old lady died the other day,' said the taxi driver.

'Yes, I believe she did.'

'You a relation?'

She stared at the house, feeling the ebb and flow of so many emotions reaching parts she'd assumed long dead. 'Yes, I am.'

'Are you going to get that great heap?' He shook his head. 'Sure wouldn't want to have to pay for the repair of that roof. Hope she left a bag full of money.'

She smiled nervously. She had no idea what her aunt had

left to Freddie. But it was clear he would need to spend a lot of money if Scorrier House was to look like a happy home again. 'Me too,' she said as she paid him, hoping that Freddie would be in. Otherwise she would have to walk to the village and call a taxi. She didn't know where she would go next, but she knew she needed to find Max too, and apologise. Not that he would want to set eyes on her again, but she had to try. She owed him that, at the very least.

'Happy Christmas,' the taxi driver called, and she turned and waved at him. For the first time in years, she firmly hoped it was going to be a happy Christmas. Walking slowly up to the front door, she wondered what she would find. Would her aunt still be 'in residence', or with the undertakers? Would Freddie be alone? And could he forgive her? How could she have been so rude to him last night on the phone? She closed her eyes for a moment and said a silent prayer for strength.

The large front door loomed, with its lion's-head knocker. The eyes glinted in the sun. Abby took a deep breath, then knocked three times. She took a step back. The red paint had lost its gloss and had peeled around the edges.

At first she heard nothing, but then the sounds of Christmas carols reached her. She waited another few minutes before walking to the back of the house. As she had seen with the Ghost of Christmas Present, the garden, except for the beds next to the house, was in a terrible state. The ground sloped down towards the basement kitchen and Abigail saw that the door was ajar. A solid baritone was singing along to 'Deck the Halls'. Freddie was here – although she still had trouble associating this deep voice with her sister's son.

Abigail looked heavenward and mouthed, 'Jaks, I'm so sorry I let you down, but I promise to be a better person . . . the person you entrusted your son to.'

'Hello,' she called.

Freddie stopped singing in mid *fa la la la la*. He turned and a smile spread across his face.

'Abby.' He stopped and stared. She wanted to move but understood that he needed time. She must look like the ghost of his past, the one that abandoned him.

'Happy Christmas, Freddie.' She took a small step towards him, trying not to cry. He opened his arms wide and she was embraced in a bear-like hug. It was the reverse of all the hugs she remembered. But even then he had hugged fiercely, afraid that if he let go the person would leave him. She had broken her promise to him so badly.

'Now, this is the best Christmas present.' He dropped his arms. 'Thank you for coming. I'd hoped you would.'

She could see the tears pooling in his eyes and knew hers were already flowing. 'Freddie, I'm so . . . sorry.' She wiped her eyes. 'For everything.'

His big brown eyes – so like Jaks' – smiled. 'It's all a bit over-whelming and well . . .' He cleared his throat. 'And with it being Christmas, none of my friends could come. They had to be with their families.' He swallowed, and she watched his Adam's apple rise and fall in his throat. He looked so grown up, but yet he was only eighteen.

Abigail followed Freddie up the stairs. The inside of the house was not as bad as she had feared. Her aunt had kept it in good shape, even if it was dated. From what she could tell, nothing had changed, not even the paint on the skirting boards, since she'd lived here as a young child. She ran her hand along the banister until they reached the ground floor. Light flooded in from the many-paned windows on either side of the door. The slate flagstones gleamed dimly through the dust. How had her aunt died? Had she been alone? Abigail hoped she hadn't been, even though her aunt had ruined so much of her family's life. Abigail recalled the despair that had gripped her as she looked at the sheet that covered her body and heard the casual words of strangers telling her that she had died alone.

There would be time enough ahead to catch up on all that she had missed. All that mattered right now was that Freddie was OK. Thankfully, they had the future to make up for the past and she wouldn't waste one moment of it.

Freddie walked ahead and opened the doors to the drawing room. There stood a tall but undecorated tree. Its shape was far from perfect, but she liked its spirit with its uneven branches and fat bottom.

'It was all they had left yesterday when I was on my way back from the Chapel of Rest.' Freddie shook his head. 'I'm not sure why I bought it, except that I found photos of a past Christmas yesterday in Mum's old room. There were loads of pictures of when you were small, Abby.'

She closed her eyes, remembering those happy times. Jaks had known all about the magic of Christmas, being ten years older, but she had only made the holiday even more special for Abby. She must try to make this one a better one for Freddie. She didn't really know how he felt about Teresa.

'I wonder if the decorations are still in the attic.' She looked about the drawing room, noting the dust sheets covering the furniture. Whipping them off a wing-back chair, she watched the dust catch in the morning light.

'I haven't been up there in years.' Freddie took the covering off the sofa.

'Shall we have a look?' She grinned.

He nodded, and she followed him up the grand staircase. She paused to look at the portraits and paintings until she came to the picture of her father. 'Your grandfather.'

'Yes. I used to talk to him when she wasn't around.'

She put her hand out and touched his arm. 'I'm sorry.'

He shrugged. 'I know. You did what you could. One time when you were allowed to see me, I heard the argument.'

She shivered, remembering the blazing row she had had with Teresa. 'I'm so sorry that you heard that, and that I haven't done more.'

'You shouldn't be. You were only three years older than I am now when you became my guardian. I can't imagine being lumped with a small child.'

'I wanted you.' She touched his arm.

'I know, but she thought she knew better.' He shrugged again. 'I still read *'Twas The Night Before Christmas* in the lead-up to Christmas.'

'You still have the book?' She took a step away, studying him.

He grinned and said, 'I do.'

Abby blinked. She turned away from him, trying to control all the emotion; but then thought better of it and opened her arms to hug him once more.


The cameraman was setting up while the choir was assembling. Abby looked around and felt a tingle of excitement. The church was adorned with pine and holly, and poinsettia plants covered the altar. Each window held a candle surrounded by more greenery. How had she missed this? How had she forgotten that Cornwall was so lovely? Everything bar the poinsettias came from the fields, woods and gardens nearby. The crib was set, with only the baby Jesus missing. Tonight they would sing to welcome the birth of the Lord. They would sing their joy in a uniquely Cornish way with their voices raised in ancient tunes.

'Mrs Turner,' a voice said.

Abby turned to see a small man in clerical garb. She smiled, saying, 'She couldn't make it. I'm Abigail Scorrier.'

'I'm so thrilled that you are going to do this.' He nodded towards the choir, who were doing warm-up exercises. 'It has worried me for years that these traditions would be lost because the young do not know them.' He shook his head. 'So few churches still sing the repeats. I have scoured the Duchy to find the arrangements and pulled singers from every part of it.'

Abigail turned her head to take a quick look at the chattering group dressed solemnly. Yet each person wore some little bit of Christmas cheer . . . from small Christmas trees to glowing baubles.

'With your programme, I hope we can reach the young. They rarely come to churches, but if they knew it was part of their heritage, then maybe we could excite the pride in them. If it weren't for Cornwall, we would all have lost some of our Christmas traditions.'

Abby nodded. 'Would you mind saying that all again, to the camera?'

'Not at all.' He stood a little straighter.

'Wonderful. Peter, the cameraman, will be ready in a few minutes. In the meantime, I'll have a word with a few of the singers to see how they feel about it.'

She reached the nave of the church as the choirmaster arrived. There was a cheer that greeted him. Abigail stopped in her tracks. Sunlight fell through the windows and played off his red hair. It was still long enough to curl slightly at the neck and by his ears. She rubbed her thumb and fingers together, remembering twirling the hair around her fingers and watching the colour change shade as it curved.

She stood two feet behind him as he tapped his baton on the podium. 'We are to be filmed today during rehearsal and for part of the service of Boxing Day.' His head moved as he scanned the choir. Abigail did the same. On one side she saw the beautiful soprano again. She shouldn't be surprised, but she was.

'This is our chance to shine and to show the world that Cornwall is more than ice cream and pasties, no matter how good they are. Sophie Turner will interview some of you.'

She took two steps closer. This would hurt him as much as it would her. Everything in her wanted to run away. She had caused him so much pain.

'I think she's here.' Someone pointed to her.

Abigail opened her mouth, then shut it again as Max turned with a big smile. It fell away as he lost all the colour in his face. His eyes appeared over-large and suddenly sad.

'Hello, Max. Sophie couldn't make it, so I'm afraid you're stuck with me.'

'Abby,' he breathed out, and she barely heard the word, but knew the whole choir was watching with fascination. This was not the time for apologies or explanations.

'Max, there's so much I need to say, but right now we both have a job to do.'

He nodded curtly as the cameraman walked towards them.


The windows in the car had fogged up the moment she got in. Abigail couldn't remember when she had last been this bone-weary. It was one in the morning. Midnight Mass was over. Filming was finished until Boxing Day. Resting her head on the wheel, she thought of the drive back to Scorrier House. Freddie was waiting, but she hoped he wasn't. He had laughed when she said he should go to bed, but he too had gone to midnight Mass. He understood she had to do her job and would have come with her, but there was this girl he met in the pub. She smiled, thinking of him telling her about Samantha. Young love.

Max hadn't done or said more than what was absolutely necessary to her in the course of the filming. He was the ulti-mate professional. She respected that, and she knew he might not want or need to hear her words of apology. The whole evening in Manaccan had gone as she had seen it with the ghost, but she had now lived it – the difference being that she could make things better for the people around her. Everywhere she smiled, held open doors, let people ahead in the queue and wished everyone a happy Christmas.

She would have to wait until Boxing Day to speak to Max, and if he didn't want to listen, then she would leave it. Despite what she had seen, he had moved on and that was good. She must build a new life.

There was a tap on the window. Abigail jumped and squealed, thinking of all sorts of terrors. Then she remembered where she was: a small village in Cornwall. It was Christmas Day 2016 and she opened the door.

'Sorry to scare you.' It was Hannah, one of the teen singers. 'I forgot to give you this note.' She smiled. 'Max had to dash to get to his parents'. Sorry I forgot, but so pleased you haven't left yet.' She handed over the envelope. 'Merry Christmas and see you tomorrow.' She dashed off to join a group.

Abigail looked at her name written in Max's bold scrawl. She turned it over, wondering if it told her to get lost, as well it should.

*Abby, or should it be Abigail now?*
*It's probably just as well that I had to leave immediately to head to my parents'. Seeing you has brought up a great deal of anger. I know we need to speak. Meet me on our beach tomorrow at four.*

She folded the note and slipped it back into the envelope. It's a good thing she and Freddie were having an early lunch with the neighbour.


The sun was setting, and the wind had a bite to it. Abby pulled her coat tighter and nestled her head down into the scarf at her neck. The clear slice of the moon hung above the cliff behind them. Max stood staring at the waves breaking on the beach. They'd walked in awkward silence from the car park.

Eventually he turned. 'Why now?'

She longed to move closer to him, liking the definition that age had brought to his face. His cheekbones were more pronounced. In fact, he was thinner and dressed smarter than she remembered, and in that moment she knew she loved him more than she ever had.

'Fate.'

'Fate?'

'Yes, Sophie being unable to travel forced me back home.'

Abby pulled the scarf higher up her face. Now was the time of truth. 'I wouldn't have come otherwise. Although now it pains me to say that.'

'Why?'

'I had . . .' Abby chewed her lips. How to explain what had happened on the train and not sound completely insane. 'I had a St Paul moment, where I was knocked off my horse good and hard and somehow sense returned.'

His eyes appeared so sad. 'I'm pleased for you.'

'Thank you.'

He stood a foot away from her, and the incoming tide was not far from his feet. She put her hand up but then dropped it down to her side. 'I'm sorry.'

He turned to look at her.

'For all the pain, the lost years and, well, everything. I don't know why you stayed with me so long.'

'Don't you?' He took one step closer to her and she could see the last arc of light from the sunset hit his hair and catch the flecks of gold in his eyes.

'No. I wasn't worthy of you or your love.'

'Yes, you were. You were the bravest, most loving person I'd ever met, but then you changed.'

Abby nodded.

'Your need to succeed and prove your aunt wrong became everything, your ambition was all.' He turned away. 'I've followed your career. You've done well.'

'In my career, yes, but at what cost? I lost everything. Despite the hard work and the money, I never got Freddie back. I lost you. I lost my soul.'

'There are some things that you can have again.' The water was almost at his feet. They would have to move when the next big wave broke.

'Anything that was worth something from my past is gone. Freddie isn't Freddie any longer, but an independent young man. You.' The waves broke, and they both dashed up the beach together.

'I'm still here. I haven't gone away.'

Abby turned and looked at their footprints being washed away as each wave brought the water higher up the beach. The cliffs around them were caught in the golden light, softening the edges of the rocks.

'Max.' She turned, and he was so close to her. Her heart beat so loudly she couldn't think. 'Please tell me you have moved on.' She took a breath. 'I don't think I could bear it if you hadn't. Maybe the beautiful soprano?'

A slow smile spread across his face. 'You're jealous.'

She nodded.

'That's Gabe Blythe. Let's call her my muse. But she has never been more than that.' He laughed dryly. 'If by moving on you meant did I have other girlfriends, then yes. For a while I hated you, really tried to get you of my system. Then I realised that wasn't helping.' He gave a sad smile. 'It wasn't even covering up what I really felt . . . the anger, the powerlessness.' He shoved his hands in his pockets but then pulled them out again. 'But if you meant did I stop loving you, then no, although I gave it my best shot.'

'No.' Abby blinked and turned away. The love in his eyes hurt.

He took her face gently into his hands and held it so she couldn't look away. 'I love you, Abigail Scorrier. I always have, and I always will. That will not change, ever.' His thumb brushed the tears trailing down her cheek. She didn't deserve his love.

He bent and slowly pressed his lips against hers. She wanted to pull away but couldn't. She was home. Every nerve in her body was alive again. She kissed him back and as the water reached their feet, he took her hand and ran with her up the beach.

'Happy Christmas, Abby.'

In the distance they heard carollers. They walked arm and arm to join them. Singing, they strolled along until they reached the pub. She wasn't sure if she wanted to be with other people, but the goodwill around then beckoned them onwards. A Christmas tree sparkled in the corner and she wondered if this was a dream. How could Max still love her after what she had done? Looking around at the happy faces, she caught sight of the blank television screen. She thought of all that Jaks had missed out on and knew she had to grab the chance she had been given with both hands. She spied a bough of mistletoe hanging from a beam and she led Max under it. 'Merry Christmas, Max. I love you.' Abby kissed him, trying to make up for all the lost years.

There was a loud cough. 'By Dickens, if it isn't Max Opie and Abby Scorrier back together again.'

Max and Abby pulled apart to see their old choirmaster standing beside the fire. 'Happy Christmas, one and all.'

# Afterword

## Cornwall and Christmas Carols

My interest in this subject began long before I set foot in Cornwall in 1989. It probably began with my father's love of the 1951 movie, *A Christmas Carol*, starring Alistair Sim as Scrooge. My father also loved to sing, especially Christmas carols. Christmas back in Massachusetts was always about singing and we even went carolling. And there was nothing better than gathering around a piano or organ and belting out the familiar songs.

When I spent my first Christmas in Cornwall in 1991, I was confronted by carols with the same words yet different tunes. The most striking of these was the popular *While Shepherds Watched Their Flocks by Night* sung to the Lyngham tune. In the part of Cornwall where I live (near the Helford) this is traditional and it's sung in rounds. I was at first puzzled and then intrigued when I first heard this sung in our local church.

Eventually this intrigue led to a rabbit hole of research into Cornwall and the Christmas carol. Christmas carols have been around a long time of course, in one form or another, from the early pagan songs through to the medieval ones. It was St.

Francis of Assisi who encouraged carols to be sung in the vernacular so that people understood what they were singing about. In the United Kingdom during the Puritan years, Christmas and the associated singing was actually banished for they considered it was a pagan festival. But thankfully royalist Cornwall was too remote, and the locals continued to sing. And it must be said that the Cornish have always held Christmas in their hearts. When you get the Cornish together, they love to sing, and Christmas gives them this opportunity. In our area alone there are normally four or five public carol singing events, not counting the ones in churches.

The carols we know so well today mostly came from the Victorian era. But this wouldn't have happened without the work of one Cornish man, Davies Giddy (also known as Davies Gilbert but that is another story), of St Erth. In 1822 he published a collection of just eight carols that he recalled from his childhood because he felt they were in danger of dying out. What he did was extraordinary. His publication, *Some Ancient Christmas Carols,* revived these carols that would otherwise have been lost. It went to a second edition the following year, including twelve more carols along with *The Helston Foray* (The Furry Dance). William Sandys, another man married to a Cornish woman, published another collection of carols in 1833. There were over one hundred carols in that publication, and half of them were from Cornwall. These two men led the resurgence of Christmas carols that followed into the Victorian era. In Cornwall this was embraced with Methodism and the local composer and miner, Thomas Merritt. Carol signing grew and grew.

Cornwall is also responsible for the now popular Christmas service of *Nine Lessons and Carols.* This service is commonly associated with King's College, Cambridge, but its real origin is attributed to the bishop of Cornwall, Edward White Benson, who in 1880 devised the service to keep his flock out of the pubs on Christmas Eve while Truro cathedral was being built. Knowing how the Cornish love to sing and love Christmas this was a cunning plan!

Of course, it was the miners who took their carols with them wherever they went overseas. When researching this novella I sourced a collection from as far away as Australia. But they are found anywhere the miners went. So, the impact of the Cornish on Christmas and the carols we associate with it is huge.

When I first wrote this novella in 2016 there were very few sources of information and happily this has now changed. The wonderful book *Hark! The Glad Sound of Cornish Carols,* by Hillary Coleman and Sally Burley, is a wonderful resource for anyone who wishes to know more about this fascinating history.

# Author's Note

After I had written the words 'the end' on *A Cornish Stranger* the character of Max Opie stayed with me. I confess I was a little bit in love with him and wanted him to find his happy ever after. So on many plot walks he would pop up in my head. Just what was Max's back story. Who had broken his heart?

Because Max was a musician it felt right to use the framework of Dickens's *A Christmas Carol* with its staves and ghosts. I have always loved this story in its many versions especially the Muppets's unique approach. In our family it is not to be missed even if we also watch another adaptation as well.

One night while on Great Western Railway's Night Riviera sleeper train, the story came together. The ghosts would appear during the course of the overnight journey and give Abigail Scorrier the chance to amend her ways and to apologise to Max.

Christmas in Cornwall is rather special with its unique variations of Christmas Carols and as the birth place of the Nine Lessons and Carols. I also wanted to tell the story of how Cornwall helped to save the Christmas Carol. I hope this little Cornish twist on the classic tale brings you a dollop of Christmas cheer.

If you are curious to read more of Max's journey and some of the other characters in the novella.... then you may want to read my novel, *A Cornish Stranger,* published in 2015 and available on Amazon or through bookshops.

# Acknowledgments

My first thanks have to go to Mr Dickens. *A Christmas Carol* is a story that has never grown old. When I was writing *A Cornish Stranger*, Max Opie wouldn't leave me. I had to know his story. Why was he writing such a heart-wrenching libretto using the Lovers of Porthgwarra? Then Christmas rolled around and our family watched *The Muppet Christmas Carol* as we always do... Max's story was born then; or more correctly, Abby's was.

Huge thanks to Carole Blake, my agent, who sadly left this world while I was finishing this novella. She was my friend, mentor, agent, and a wonderful person. I shall be lost without her. Harriet Bourton, my editor, and all at team Orion have been wonderful. My crucial support crew of Brigid Coady, Christine Moriarty, Sarah Callejo, and my family deserve awards for putting up with me.

But the biggest thanks goes to my readers . . .

# About the Author

Called '*the queen of the contemporary Cornish novel*' by the Guardian, Liz is the author of nine books and two novellas, including the most recent *The Secret Shore* which was short-listed for the Historical Romantic Novel Award 2024 from the Romantic Novelists' Association. She lives with her husband and two mad cats near the Helford River in Cornwall. When not writing Liz is reading, painting, knitting and procrastinating on social media.

Her books are available in English, Swedish, Dutch, German, Portuguese, French, Estonian, Norwegian, Danish, Turkish, Latvian, Serbian, Czech, Hungarian, Italian and Finnish.

If you would like to subscribe to Liz's newsletter, sign up via her website at lizfenwick.com.

Follow Liz Fenwick on:

facebook.com/liz.fenwick

x.com/@liz_fenwick

instagram.com/liz_fenwick

tiktok.com/@lizfenwickauthor

Printed in Great Britain
by Amazon

54697493R00057